The Inheritance of Exile

Stories from South Philly

Susan Muaddi Darraj

University of Notre Dame Press

Notre Dame, Indiana

Published by the University of Notre Dame Press
Notre Dame, Indiana 46556
www.undpress.nd.edu

Library of Congress Cataloging in-Publication Data

Darraj, Susan Muaddi.
The inheritance of exile : stories from South Philly / Susan Muaddi Darraj.
p.   cm.
ISBN-13: 978-0-268-03503-7 (pbk. : alk. paper)
ISBN-10: 0-268-03503-2 (pbk. : alk. paper)
1. Arab American women—Fiction.   2. Mothers and daughters—Fiction.
3. South Philadelphia (Philadelphia, Pa.)—Fiction.   I. Title.
PS3604.A75I54   2007
813'.6—dc22
                              2007002523

The
Inheritance
of Exile

For
Elias & Mariam

- Melancolic,
fatalistic tone
- Contrasts of old world to
New world.

Contents

HANAN

REEMA

Acknowledgments

As a fellow writer recently told me, "Having a short story collection published is no mean thing in this age of the blockbuster novel." How true. I owe thanks to Barbara Hanrahan at the University of Notre Dame Press for e-mailing me in the spring of 2006 to say she loved my stories, to Rebecca DeBoer for helping me polish and shape the manuscript, and to Margaret Gloster for including my ideas as she worked on the book's design.

I am grateful to the members of my writing group: Lalita Noronha, Barbara Westwood Diehl, Meredyth Santangelo, Lara McLaughlin, Patricia Schultheis, Rosalia Scalia, Susan McCallum-Smith, and Andria Cole. We have been meeting monthly for three years, and they have been my first audience for nearly every story here.

It is difficult to describe the immense debt I owe my family: my parents, Bassam and Alice Muaddi, and my brothers,

Aboud, Jawad, and Samy Muaddi; my husband, Elias Darraj; and my daughter, Mariam. My growth as a writer is deeply rooted in their love and support.

Some of these stories have appeared in the same or a slightly different form in the following publications:

"Back to the Surface," *New York Stories*, Spring 2001.

"The New World," *Dinarzad's Children: An Anthology of Contemporary Arab American Fiction,* edited by Pauline Kaldas and Khaled Mattawa (Fayetteville: University of Arkansas Press, November 2004).

"Aliyah's Fan," *Mizna,* December 2001.

"Preparing a Face," *The Orchid Literary Review,* November 2004, Issue 4.

"Sufficing," *Mizna,* Spring 2003.

NADIA

Back to the Surface

Nobody believed what I said about Siti, not even my mother. Maybe she didn't want to accept it, maybe it was too painful, like opening your eyes to the yellow glare of the midday sun, so she resisted.

"Nadia, your grandmother is dead," my mother said, soothing me back to sleep. She knelt on the floor, hovering over my bed, stroking my hair along my back the way she used to when, as a child of twelve, I cried for my father. A drunk driver had hit him that year, but it took him three months to die in the hospital. "They'll have to take me kicking and screaming," he'd promise, lying still in his hospital bed, in too much pain to even clasp my hand. But he left without a sound.

Now my mother smoothed my hair again in long, comforting strokes that ended in the middle of my back, before starting again at the top of my head, like a skier at the summit of a steep slope. Except that now I was twenty-one and seeing visions of my grandmother.

"But I saw her," I repeated stubbornly, my shoulders still shaking. I'd awakened, screaming, minutes earlier, prompting my mother to burst in from her adjoining bedroom.

"What did she say?" she asked, patiently. Nervously.

"Nothing," I sighed. I knew she wouldn't believe me or, worse, would try to argue with me, begging me to "be logical." "Go back to bed—we're both tired. I'm fine now."

M y father had never spoken to me again after he died, though I willed him to. Many nights that year, I'd lie attentively in bed, conjuring up his image in my mind. Not as he looked in the coffin—pale and pasty, the mortician's makeup job masking his smooth olive skin—but as he looked when he played baseball with me or as he sang songs during road trips to entertain Mama and me. Since I was always in the backseat, I could only glimpse his mustache and lips in the rearview mirror, sometimes his white teeth when he smiled, pleased at how well he'd delivered a particular verse. So his half-face is what I frequently imagined, though it never spoke to me, only gazed at me sadly, apologetically, lips pressed together.

On the other hand, my grandmother arrived in my dreams the same night that she died—she flew in quietly and settled into the brightest corner of my mind. She wore her pale blue housedress, its large pockets weighed down with her large bundle of keys, her packet of cigarettes, chapstick, quarters for the washing machine, and the eyeglasses that she refused to wear. They were unusable anyway, having been badly scratched by the constant companionship of sharp-edged keys. Her face was rolled into a quiet smile that would often unravel into a sneaky grin, reminding me of the times she allowed me a clandestine reprieve from my punishments as soon as my mother left our apartment. Siti's hands smelled salty, like the brine of the grape leaves she was eternally stuffing and rolling at the kitchen table while listening to her tapes of Om Kulthoum in concert. "That

4

woman had a voice, God bless her," she would say, shaking her head in amazement, her fingers working quickly and steadily, stacking the completed grape leaves in piles before her, like an arsenal of snowballs on a winter afternoon.

The first night she appeared, she said, "I'm sorry that I didn't wait for you."

"Mama's still upset," I replied. We had to hurry to the hospital when the nurse called, but Siti had died before we reached her room. I could tell immediately upon entering the cold room that we were too late, from her closed eyes and the way her mouth drooped open. Mama looked as if she'd been betrayed.

"You have to help her, *habibti*," Siti said, touching my lips with her fingers. I could taste the salt on her skin and see the green stains from the leaves on her cuticles, outlining her wide, square nails. I also recognized the added acidic taste of the lemon that she used to scrub out the stains. I liked when she called me *habibti*, "my love" in Arabic. I'm the only grandchild she said that to, maybe because I was the oldest and resembled her the most.

"OK, but come back," I said. She grinned and left, and I didn't cry two days later when we buried her, even though all my aunts beat their foreheads and wailed and my uncles sobbed into their hands like children. They had flown in from Jerusalem for the funeral, arguing that their mother should be buried back home. But Mama, exhausted from crying and lack of sleep, had hysterically insisted that Siti be buried here, in Philadelphia, because she'd come with Aunt Nadia to live with us when Baba died. "She wouldn't want to leave us now."

As we wearily watched them lower her coffin into the cold ground, Mama was amazed at my calmness. "It's OK to cry," she told me, holding me tightly. "We all miss her—it's OK to cry." I nodded, not knowing how to tell her that she had misunderstood.

I was named after my youngest aunt, Nadia, who was only eleven when my mother married my father. My father always liked the name because, in Arabic, it meant "the dew on the flower's petal," and he loved that image. "Only the Arabs give their kids names that are pictures," he would boast, half-seriously, half-jokingly. So I became "little Nadia" in the extended circle of the family. After Baba died, Nadia the Elder, who'd been in her twenties and the only one still unmarried, moved with Siti to the States to live with us.

At thirty, she had married a "non-Arab," as he became known among the family, who also referred to him simply as "Nadia's husband," or more often, "*al-Amerikani*." But his real name was Kevin and he was an Irish-American, tall and blond and handsome. When I say "tall," I mean 6 feet 4 inches, not what Arabs refer to as tall, which could be anything from 5 feet 8 inches and above. He had a large, welcoming smile and bright blue eyes that he passed on to their son, Patrick. With those eyes, Patrick could charm anything out of any member of the family of dark-eyed Arab-Americans who adored him but were wary of his father.

Actually, Siti was the most suspicious and she spread her bad vibes to the rest of us. "He won't understand our culture," she'd insisted when she realized that Nadia and Kevin were becoming a serious couple, when they were seen together at every party and event, so conspicuous because of the contrast in their heights and looks.

"Mama," Nadia would begin to argue and then trail off as if she were too exhausted to continue. She would come to the apartment, sip many cups of dark coffee with my mother, and talk for hours in the kitchen. Sometimes I would join them, but when the conversation became very serious, Mama beckoned for me to leave. Nadia the Elder would apologize with a wink to soothe my insulted feelings.

She married Kevin despite the frown that Siti wore throughout the entire church ceremony. I was actually thrilled for Nadia, but dared not act too exuberant in front of Siti. Things calmed down when Patrick was born two years later and he glittered our lives with his laughter. He was only four years old when Siti died. She told me in a dream weeks later how much she especially hated leaving him. "Promise to spoil him," she entreated me and I agreed solemnly.

A few months after Siti died, when Patrick was five and newly in
school and I was newly in love and Mama had finally stopped wearing black, I noticed that Nadia the Elder had stopped being happy.
She rarely smiled anymore and became very protective of Patrick,
clinging to him tightly. Often, she showered him with a frightening
excess of kisses, so fiercely that a few times he grew uncomfortable,
pulling away from her.

I returned home from work one night, having dealt with some
hard-to-please clients at the agency. As I climbed the steps and unlocked the door, I thought about my date with George later that
night—we were supposed to see a Japanese film at the Ritz Theater.
The sound of Patrick's happy babbling surprised me as I swung open
my front door.

My aunt sat at the kitchen table with my mother. They both
looked anxious, strained, their thick, dark brows weaved together at
the center of their foreheads. "Siham, you're just as old-fashioned as
Mama," Nadia the Elder was saying. Then they both glanced up and
saw me.

"What's up?" I asked, hesitating in the kitchen's entrance. My
mother had a secret language with her sisters that I, as an only child,
did not understand. The rules often had to be spelled out for me
simply and clearly.

"Nothing," they both said, my signal to go upstairs and get ready
for my evening out. The expression on their faces was clear enough,
so I showered, dressed, and left, slipping Patrick a handful of candy
as I made my stealthy exit.

When I came home later, I checked for Nadia's car on the street,
but it was nowhere to be seen. "She's gone," I told George, who leaned
in for a kiss, just as I glimpsed my mother watching from the second-
story window, her face half-concealed by the lacy green curtain. I
pushed George away and rolled my eyes upward toward the window.
He followed my look in time to see my mother's silhouette vanish.

"She's crafty," he said with a smile. He had a lot of respect for my
mother. When he'd been a student, new from Syria, she had invited

him over to our house for dinner, cooking his favorite dishes, like *warak dawali* and *magloubeh*. But he also knew she was paranoid about me.

"She's not there now," he added, kissing me anyway. My front door opened behind us but, absorbed in our kiss, we failed to notice until my mother spoke.

"Nadia, I need to speak to you inside," she said loudly.

Springing back, George mumbled, *"Masel khair, Sitt Jundi,"* as he straightened the collar of his shirt.

"Good evening? George, it's two o'clock in the morning," she replied brusquely. "And I need to speak to my daughter."

Squeezing his arm, I followed Mama inside and immediately began apologizing. For what, I wasn't sure, but I felt from her expression that I ought to be sorry.

She waved her hand dismissively. "Nadia, you're too old for that—I don't care what you do. I really do need to talk to you." She headed upstairs to her bedroom and opened the window to let in some fresh, clean air. "Your aunt is having serious problems." She took a pillow and laid it on the sill, then leaned her elbows on it and stared up into the city's night sky. I joined her, anticipating a long talk, which we frequently had, sitting just like this on nights when neither one of us could sleep. We'd started almost immediately after my father had died, huddled in the window like a couple of crones, shoulders hunched as if bracing ourselves for another punch. The streets were quiet, and even our neighbors downstairs seemed to have understood that they should be silent tonight. When I was a child, there was a flower shop below us, but the owner had died and her daughter had quickly sold it. After many permutations, including a Vietnamese grocery store and a short-lived espresso café, it was now a used CD and record shop, with customers coming in and playing and listening to music until late at night. The Polish and Vietnamese families who lived on either side of us were quiet tonight as well, perhaps lulled to sleep by the crisp air that made you want to burrow under layers of blankets.

"What's wrong with her?" I asked, leaning far out to try to glimpse George walking back up the street. But the night was too black, too opaque to be pierced by the street lamp's feeble light.

"She wants to divorce Kevin."

That stunned me back to attention. I turned to look at her and noticed how much older she seemed. Her brown eyes were rimmed with red and her dark hair fell limply, lifelessly around her shoulders. She wore one of my grandmother's old housedresses, one from Jerusalem with the red and blue embroidered panel on the bust. Days after Siti's funeral, my aunts and mother had divided up her clothes and jewelry among themselves. My aunts vied for her bracelets and necklaces, her silver brooch and her colorful scarves. My mother hoarded, almost obsessively, all of her housedresses and even her old leather house slippers. Mama used to wear colorful clothing, fashionable stuff, but lately all she wore were those shabby dresses. The thread's once-bright, vibrant colors were faded now, and I suddenly realized that my mother resembled Siti in the last year of her life.

"She says she doesn't love him anymore—she just fell out of love. I can't believe she's doing this to him—and to her son."

The fingers of my mother's left hand clenched in a tight fist, then relaxed, clenched and released again. I knew she was furious because Nadia was treating marriage so casually, and especially since her marrying Kevin had originally sparked such a commotion in the family.

"It's because she's the youngest," my mother continued. "Your grandparents spoiled her the way they never spoiled the rest of us— whatever she wanted, she got it. They never wanted to upset her.

"She was sick, too, when she was young. Always had chest colds and high fevers—she stayed in bed for a whole month one time because your grandfather didn't have enough money to let her stay at the hospital. It was during the war and the beds were filled with people who were getting amputations and recovering from shrapnel and gunshot wounds. He was a doctor, so he treated her at home as well as he could. Your Siti didn't sleep at all that month—she kept checking Nadia's temperature, boiling sage and chamomile with honey, making cold compresses for her head and warm ones for her belly. And she grew up that way, knowing that your grandmother and everyone would do what she wanted."

She was quiet for a few seconds and then both fists clenched and slammed down on the pillow, which muffled their impact.

"Damn her!"

She left, went to bed, but I stayed by the window, sorting out this new information.

I knew that my mother was hurting, but when her hurt spilled over into anger, it was my signal that she was thinking about my father. Unavoidable parallels between Nadia's marriage and her own stolen one were probably burrowing steadily into her mind. After a few minutes had passed quietly, I smoothed the two dents in the pillow with my palm, closed the window, and went to bed.

Nadia the Elder did not come to our house for six weeks, but my mother had tense phone conversations with her. She sat at the kitchen table, a full cup of coffee, long grown cold, before her, her mouth pressed close to the receiver, and she spoke in low, terse Arabic. Sometimes, I could hear her voice rise and once I heard her say, "If our mother was alive, she'd never let you do this!" That particular conversation ended shortly thereafter, but my mother stayed at the table, staring down at the pine wood surface, tracing invisible circles with her thumb.

I told George what was going on—said that I wanted to hang out at home more often in case my mother needed me. He smiled and held me for a long time, as if to send his strength to me that way, and he reminded me about the skiing trip that weekend. "I forgot—oh, George, I probably shouldn't."

"We promised Hanan and John we'd go with them. Besides, a couple days in the Poconos will help you forget these troubles."

I finally, reluctantly, said I would go. But the night before the trip, my grandmother visited me, wearing a stern, disturbed expression.

"Are you upset about Nadia?" I asked her. This was the first time she'd come to me since I'd heard the news.

She ignored me, ignored the question, and told me instead that I shouldn't go on the trip with George. "You don't know what could happen," she said.

"Siti, George is a nice guy. Mama likes him—we might even get engaged soon."

She didn't reply, just shook her head and clicked her tongue.

I assured her that we were going with a group of friends, that we'd be safe, that she didn't have to worry about *a-naas*. A-naas is a phrase that I had often heard her fret over: "What will *a-naas* say?" "What will *a-naas* think?" She always worked herself into a frenzy about the gossip circles created and perpetuated by *a-naas*, the small but organized network of Arab women and men in America who had the uncanny ability to transmit a single, juicy nugget of information about someone's reputation across the Atlantic Ocean and the Mediterranean Sea to the corresponding family network back in the Middle East.

She left me that night, still agitated despite my reassurances. I told her, just before she faded, that my mother did not see a problem with the trip.

"She doesn't think now," she answered, "not clearly," and was gone.

"Mama, are you OK with the trip I'm going on tonight?"

"The trip with George?" she asked, leaning all her strength into scrubbing the large pot in the sink. She had made *mansaff* last night for some friends, and they'd all ooh-ed and aah-ed appreciatively as she'd laid the flat dish on the table, the mound of fluffy rice atop a foundation of shredded pita bread, quilted with roasted almond slivers and slabs of juicy lamb meat, all drenched in the milky *laban*. The guests had left late, so neither of us had done the dishes and now, the *laban*—everyone's favorite part of the meal—had stuck to the side of the pot in flaky, cellulite-like ridges. My mother was on her second Brillo pad, pearls of sweat breaking through the defenses of her hairline.

"Yes, the one to the Poconos. We're leaving early in the morning."

"To the what?" She shut off the faucet and I realized how noisy the water had been—and how eerily quiet it was now. "Where is the trip?"

"To the Poconos. We're going skiing with Hanan and John."

"OK, *habibti*. That's fine, as long as you and Hanan sleep in one room and you let George and the American boy stay in another room." She resumed her scrubbing, water off, using a pool of water that had collected in the belly of the pot. "I told you that I like George." She smiled at me, a sad, small smile. "I hope that you marry him someday—he's a good man. He'd never leave you or . . . hurt you. Some men hurt the people they love without even knowing it, but not George. He's different."

"I know." I sat at the kitchen table and started to dry the water glasses that she'd just washed.

"Every woman needs a man to be with, not for money or anything, but for friendship. For love."

"Yes, I know."

"And I hope that you would never leave him or hurt him, like your aunt is doing to Kevin." She wiped her forehead with the red sleeve of her housedress. Her elbow knocked the blue stone that dangled from the shelf above the sink, dropping it into the suds in the sink. She picked it up carefully and replaced it. "Good men are rare, Nadia."

"I think Siti is not convinced of that," I hazarded after a few moments.

"What did you say?" She interrupted her scrubbing once again to stare at me.

"Siti. She told me last night, in my dream," I continued. "She doesn't want me to go." I pushed the dishcloth deep into the mouth of the glass, swiveling it around with my index and middle fingers, left then right, snatching up every drop of moisture. "I think she doesn't trust him completely."

Before I knew what was happening, before I could glimpse the metamorphosis of her expression, Mama snatched the glass out of my hand and smashed it against the blue and white tiles of the wall. Her black eyes were twin pools of fury, rippled with fear, I thought, as I sat stunned in my chair.

"Goddamnit, Nadia!" she shrieked. "Your grandmother is dead!"

I didn't say a word as she stomped out of the kitchen, crushing the glass shards into powder underneath her wooden house sandals.

"Why do you keep torturing me like this, goddamnit!" she screamed from the hallway. After the door to her bedroom slammed shut, I swept up the glass, then finished scrubbing the pot.

I packed that night and then hung out in the kitchen, hoping Mama would come out of her room. Eventually, I gave up and slept for a few hours, and listened intently to any sounds from next door. I heard nothing. Early the next morning, she still hadn't emerged, so I left for the trip without saying goodbye.

The last thing I remembered before we crashed was that George reached out for my hand, his other hand still on the wheel, and . . . yes, then Hanan and John screamed from the backseat. And then— or maybe it was before they screamed—the flash of headlights, of someone else's headlights to my right, blinding me before it all went black.

I sank to the bottom of a dark blue ocean, the floor littered with thousands of eyes and lips, staring, speaking, confusing me. Blue eyes, brown eyes. Lips that spoke in Arabic and English. One mouth in particular intrigued me—a pair of bright, green lips that opened wide, large enough for me to swim through. Tired and too sleepy to think, I drifted toward it, not moving really, just floating and letting it pull me in.

And then a warm grip on my ankle and I was being pulled away, too weary to turn back and see who this other force was, pulling me up through miles and years of water, back to the surface. Only then, when the bright sky beckoned me to open my eyes and energized me, I saw Siti, cradling my head in her elbow and stroking my hair back, away from my eyes, from my cheeks and lips.

"Go back," she said. "Don't come here yet."

I opened my mouth to speak, but no sound pierced the still, quiet air. Mute and suddenly scared, I stared at her.

"Tell your aunt to be a mother. Tell her to be a loyal wife." She paused. "And say that Kevin is good."

I nodded, clutching my throat. Her words, her tone, the rhythm of her voice, resounded in my skull, sticking to it like the dried ridges of laban *to the pot.*

"And your mother must forgive your aunt. Help her to be happy." She called me habibti *and stared into my face, as if assigning me to a mission, putting her trust in me. "Help her because I cannot."*

She pressed my cheeks together between her warm palms and kissed my eyes, saying "Go back," then sank below the blue waters.

When I awoke, I was lying in a white bed, surrounded by the anxious faces of George, my mother, my friends and their mothers, and Nadia the Elder, who sat in a corner, clutching Patrick in her lap. Hanan's mother stood clutching the crucifix around her neck, mumbling, "He's brought them back, He's brought them back." My mother said nothing, but she held my hand so tightly and kissed my forehead so fervently that I thought perhaps she understood or, at least now, she would be willing to listen.

The New World

It was a small apartment, comprising the second and third stories of the row house; the first level was a flower shop, run by an Italian widow and her spinster daughter. On Siham's first day in the apartment, they had brought up a co-conut custard pie, slightly browned on top. It had also been her first week in America, so they gave her a red rose as well. Mrs. Donato spoke with a heavy accent, which reassured Siham about her own. But Carla, the daughter with the bull-ish, round eyes and the penciled eyebrows, emitted negative vibes that Siham could not explain.

The floors of the apartment were what Nader called "hardwood"—dark, polished slats of wood, side by side like slumbering children. She'd never seen floors like this; her parents' home had marble floors in every room. In Jerusalem, all the homes, even those of the very poor, were made of stone, the most democratic of building supplies because there was plenty of it. People only used wood to create heat and build furniture. Whenever Nader was at work, Siham liked to put on her socks and slide across her new "hardwood" floors like an ice skater. She hoped Philadelphia had a real ice rink, because she'd never seen one of those either, except on TV.

Nader worked all day, five days a week, with his friend Michel, who owned a food truck and catered to the businesspeople in the city. They stood at 16th and Market Streets, crammed together in a metal cart, one frying the steaks and the other bagging the soft pretzels, from 6 A.M. until late in the evening. Nader always came home, smelling like grease, his thick mustache limp with the steam that filled up their cart. She missed him terribly during the day and offered to work with them, like Michel's wife had done before their daughter Hanan had been born. But Nader had said that his wife was a lady and he didn't want her to get dirty. "What about Michel's wife?" she asked, but Nader said that she had lived in a refugee camp and was used to the dirt. "Plus she's a little loose in her head," he added.

It was an unkind comment and it bothered Siham, because she liked Layla. Siham's father had taught her to treat everyone kindly, often stitching the wounds of villagers without taking money and even without making them feel indebted (though her mother huffed in frustration when they themselves sometimes ran out of milk and eggs). Siham liked to think that she had inherited his open heart, and she told Nader many times not to speak that way. After all, like Siham, Layla was also struggling to learn English and to get used to living here. She had been pregnant with a son, and lost him, plus Hanan was a bold child, curious and daring.

But in every other way, Nader was perfect. Once a week, he stopped at the general store on 9th Street on his way home and bought her a present. Once it was a black, satin scarf, embroidered with blue leaves on silver vines. Then a tube of her favorite Revlon lipstick, a dark burgundy shimmer. It used to cost her thirty shekels, or ten dollars, in Jerusalem's finest drug stores. Here, in America, it was only two dollars at Eckerd. The most amusing things he bought her were Barbie dolls, the most American toy of all, with their long blonde plastic hair. The most thoughtful thing was a personal date book to keep her appointments, though for now those would be things like "Monday: Wash windows and dust ceiling fan" and "Thursday: Shine floors and do English exercises." She practiced her English like a religion; Nader had bought her a primer and an Arab-English dictionary (yet another present) and she rehearsed her verbs for at least an hour every morning.

Anticipate.

Expect.

Wait. I wait. You wait. He/she/it waits.

One August morning, she sat on her green sofa, a used one they'd bought from a consignment store. She was embroidering a small coin purse for herself, using the black and red design of the Palestinian villages. Her English book lay open on the armrest and she read the sentences aloud, especially practicing the words with the letters "p" and "v," which did not exist in the Arabic alphabet.

The phone rang, a not unwelcome disturbance. Siham slid across the floor to it, nearly colliding with the end table, eager to practice her English with another person. She hoped it would be one of those telephone survey people so she could get at least five minutes worth of their time.

"Is Nader home?" The voice was a woman's, but deep and smooth, like the chords of an *oud*.

"No. May I please take your message?"

"Who is this?"

"I am his wife."

"His wife!" Pause. "No, thanks. I'll try calling later."

Siham slid the phone back into its curved cradle. Not hearing the familiar "click," she picked it up and replaced it firmly. Later that evening, Nader told her not to worry about it. "I don't know who she is. If it's important, she'll call back."

"But she used your first name. That means she knows you."

"*Habibti*, in America, that's what they do. These telephone people, they don't use 'Mr.' and 'Mrs.' anymore. You'll get used to these little cultural things. It's how they get you not to hang up right away." He laughed nervously, and she knew it wasn't.

She looked up a new word in her dictionary that night, one that contained a "p," and she practiced it a few times. Suspect. I suspect. You suspect. He/she/it suspects.

Siham enjoyed exploring their new neighborhood, taking long, early afternoon walks through South Philadelphia. The streets were perfectly arranged, organized, like a grid. Numbers ran north and south, names ran east and west. Or was it the other way around? She and Nader lived on 9th and Passyunk, in what they called the Italian Market, but Siham felt it was an island, lonely, despite the flow of people. Layla rarely visited because the crowds were too much for her to handle her young daughter. The positive aspect of it was that Siham found everything at the Italian Market, from tomatoes to fresh coffee beans to bath towels, sold by everyone from leathery Vietnamese women to Sicilian men with mustaches like Nader's to young Irish women with green eyes and red curls scooped back into bandannas. Some of these Philadelphia people were immigrants like her, and others were the children of immigrants, having had an entire generation to adjust.

Sometimes, the Italian Market reminded her of the Old City quarter of Jerusalem, full of men yelling out the prices of vegetables and women peddling their crafts, their embroidered pillowcases and blouses. They even targeted tourists with photo frames and wall hangings that said in embroidered English, "God Bless Our Home" or "Home Is Where the Heart Is." In Jerusalem, she could bargain with the peddlers. In fact, they were insulted if you did not engage them in some level of negotiations. But in the Italian Market, the price was set. She knew because she'd once tried to talk the fruit man down two dollars. "Hey lady, no bargaining! This is already a bargain, ahw-ight?" Even this talent was taken from her here, rendered null. Nader claimed that her ability to bring prices down in the Khan al-Zeit bazaar was what had won his heart.

She was examining the leather wallets at the stand next to the entrance to the Dome of the Rock when he approached. They each bought a wallet, although she paid eight shekels and he paid fourteen. As Siham walked away, Nader called after her, "How did you do that?"

She did not answer. So he asked, "Can you come shopping with me? I have a few more things to buy today and I could use your help."

Siham took one look at his pleated trousers, linen blazer and shiny, lace-up shoes and kept walking. Ignored him, who was so obviously, as she'd thought, one of these returning American Arab nouveau riche. He probably sold bananas on the city streets in America but made himself look rich when he returned home to visit the "Old Country." Sickening. Especially when the richest man in the "Old Country" only made about $400 in American dollars a month. Her own father, a doctor, made a mere $250.

She entered one of the coffee shops and sat at a small table in the corner, reading her newspaper and sipping the bitter Turkish qahwa from the small, enameled cup. The boy shot in the riots yesterday had died last night. There were expansions planned for six more settlements, four in the West Bank. The Boutique Shahrazad was announcing another sale on evening gowns.

"May I join you?"

She looked up and saw Linen Blazer bent slightly over her table, staring eagerly at her.

"No."

With a chuckle, he sat down anyway. He ordered coffee for himself with an imperious wave of his hand. The other men in the café stared at them curiously, stopping their conversations to see who was this Amerkani sitting with the eldest daughter of Doctor Abdallah al-Medani. Aware of their scrutiny, Siham stood up and left.

What an ill-timed first meeting!, she thought to herself now. She'd dismissed him as a self-centered piece of fluff who had become lost among the casinos and dance clubs of America. Thank God he'd sought her out, asked people about her. He came to her parents' house and entertained her family by bringing boxes of sweets, giving her little sister Nadia rides on his shoulders, and by singing—he had such a deep, wonderful voice. He had especially charmed her mother by complimenting her cooking, the spice in her *falafel*, and the texture of the *laban* in her *mansaff*. One month later, after he and his family had formally asked for her hand in marriage, Siham applied for a visa to the States. Nader had recently become a citizen himself, so she filed happily as "spouse of U.S. citizen." They were going to wed. To marry. I marry. You marry. We marry.

She strolled toward Ellsworth Avenue and entered the lobby of the Lebanese Maronite church. Inside, Siham saw the two old Lebanese widows who volunteered to clean, polishing pews and vacuuming the dark, wine-colored carpets. Giving their free time to God, good hearts. They reminded her of her mother, who prowled around in her loose housedresses, attacking dust in every corner of their home. She and Nader had talked about eventually sponsoring her entire family to come to the States, because the economy was slipping faster than before and people couldn't even afford doctors. One of the widows kissed the image of the Virgin Mary as she dusted the base of the statue. Approaching the prayer stand in the foyer, Siham lit three candles, driving the slim, white tapers deep into the sand pile. One for her family, especially her mother, back home. One for Layla, to help her overcome her grief and to have another child soon. The third one for Nader, to keep him safe.

As she walked home, she thought how Nader would smile indulgently at her "voodoo," as he called it. When they'd first moved into the apartment, she had immediately set about sprinkling chrism on each wall. Mrs. Donato had nodded approvingly when she heard about the incident. "A good, good girl. Fears God," she'd said. But all Nader had wanted to do was make love in their new bed, though Siham had insisted on first driving a small nail in the wall so that she could hang a charm above their heads. It was a blue glass stone, with an eye painted on it, a charm that hung in every home in Jerusalem. "To ward off the Evil Eye," she announced proudly, as Nader tugged at her arm, pulled her down.

She entered the flower shop and headed for the back stairs, the only way to get up to her own apartment. It would be this way until the landlord decided to make a separate entrance. But Siham didn't mind so much. "Hello, Mrs. Donato," she said to the black-haired, elderly woman sitting at the counter, arms folded across her chest and eyes closed.

"Hello, *bella*," she replied, her eyes snapping open.

"I did not mean to awoke you, Mrs. Donato."

"No, no, *bella*. Iz OK." Mrs. Donato beckoned to her daughter, who was at the other end of the shop arranging flowers in a basket. "Wait, wait for Carla. There is a woman here before. Blondie woman."

"Blondie?"

"Wait for Carla. Wait, she tells you."

Carla approached them with two lilies in her hands, the long stems coiled like serpents. "Hi, Siham. How are you?"

"Fine, thank you very much."

"How is Nader?" she asked, a curious glitter in her brown eyes.

"Fine. Your mother, she said about a woman?"

"Yes, there was a woman here about an hour ago, looking for Nader. A tall, blonde woman. Red suit, linen, with black heels. Looked a little younger than me, maybe forty or forty-five years old."

"What does she say?" Siham interrupted Carla's flood of description. She liked Mrs. Donato, but Siham was wary of Carla, who was obviously very smart but who thrived on gossip, like her old aunts back home. A woman who never missed a single detail or a gesture or a look.

"She asked if Nader Jundi lived upstairs. I said yes, he does, with his wife." Carla casually snapped the heads off the lilies and Siham watched a lone, white petal float to the floor. "She asked how long you'd both been married. I said, 'I don't know,' but that you had moved in together a few months ago."

"Does she—did she leave a message?"

"No, she just left. Didn't even say thank you. Tossed her head and walked out."

"Thank you, Carla. I will see you later." Siham headed upstairs, a sick feeling creeping into her belly.

"*Bella*, have some coffee with us," Mrs. Donato called out behind her.

"No, thank you." She scaled the steps three at a time. Before she shut the door firmly behind her, she heard Mrs. Donato yell at Carla for ruining the flowers.

Later that night, she questioned Nader about it, as soon as he walked into the apartment. Her father used to say, as he furrowed his shaggy brows, that his daughter had been aptly named. Siham meant "arrows" in Arabic. Straight to the target. No deviations.

Nader was visibly startled, his eyes widened like white discs. Especially when she told him of her feeling that it was the same woman who had phoned the day before. "It was probably an old friend, *habibti*, from work or something," he said reassuringly, though he didn't stop tapping his foot through the rest of dinner. Siham felt suddenly guilty for upsetting him. That night, their frantic lovemaking knocked the blue stone off the wall. It rolled along the headboard and, before she could grasp it, shattered into fragments on the hardwood floor.

Siham heard nothing about the blonde woman for the next month. Nader's workdays grew longer, and he often came home with sagging shoulders but more bills in his wallet. "We're getting a lot of business because of the nice weather. Everyone wants to come out and buy lunch and get out of their offices." She could tell he was grateful for the work, because he sighed less heavily when he wrote checks for the bills at the beginning of the month. To pass the time, she began English classes at the community college. Her professor told her that she was one of the most advanced students in the class. She'd better be, she thought, after all her own self-tutoring.

By October the leaves on the occasional tree in South Philadelphia began to change colors. The trees in Jerusalem were mostly olive trees and they didn't change colors, as she tried to explain to Carla, who didn't seem to care. Their leaves just curled up like shrimp and died, pulled away from the branches by the harsh wind that whipped through and wrapped around the hills. But here, the leaves retained their shape, became muscular in texture and turned red, orange and gold. One autumn afternoon she slipped two leaves, a yellow one and a red one, into an envelope and mailed them to her youngest sister, Nadia, who lived at home. She also described Halloween to her, how goblins, witches, and boys with bizarre black and white face paint, claiming to be rock stars, came to the flower shop and the other stores along the Market for candy.

In November she found a way to help Nader pay the bills. She invited Carla and Mrs. Donato up to the apartment for tea one evening after they closed the shop. They praised her embroidery skills. It was not a rare talent for Palestinian women—Siham had been taught by her grandmothers—but Carla and her mother, deeply impressed, made a proposal. Siham gave them a pair of sofa pillowcases that she had stashed away in a chest to put for sale in the shop. They sold the next day, and the Donatos took orders for three more sets. "You make 'em, we'll sell 'em," said Carla, handing her thirty dollars that evening. "I'll just take a 10 percent cut. People snap them up when you say that they're hand-made." Siham requested only that they hide her work from Nader when he passed through the shop on his way up to the apartment after work. She wanted to save the money and surprise him with a gift.

The extra bedroom on the second level of the apartment became Siham's embroidery and study room. The floor was covered with yards of cloth and dozens of spools of thread: tightly-wound ribbons of red, wrapped rivers of yellow, and coils of green. They were rainbows in her hand that she could unfurl at will. Her English books were stacked in a corner underneath the sole window in the room. A lonely stuffed chair sat in the middle of the room, next to a halogen lamp. Her only desk was her lap. This room would be a nursery one day. They had decided to start trying soon. She had already lined all the Barbie dolls Nader had bought her over the past year—the doctor, the nurse, the singer, the horse jockey—on a small shelf, hoping it would bring them a girl.

She was sitting one November afternoon in this room. As she embroidered an octagonal cross-stitch pattern on a black mesh background, she listened to a Miles Davis cassette tape. It was part of her effort to be infinitely more American, like watching the news and grilling hamburgers. She would conquer jazz music just as she had the others, and her English professor had loaned her his cassette of Davis's music. She heard Carla's familiar tap on her door downstairs and she ran down to get the mail. The bundle, which grew daily as she and Nader became more "established" (and thus more susceptible to circulars and junk mailings) sat on the top step, where Carla left it every day. There was one letter in particular, addressed only to Nader, in a woman's slanted, looped script. The "J" of their last name was decorated with a large loop at the top. The return address had no name, only the street name and zip code: 1012 Chestnut Street.

She took it upstairs to her embroidery room and placed it at the foot of her chair. She resumed her work, counting stitches on the black cloth as she drove the needle in and out, leaving tiny footprints of bright red thread. It would be a wall hanging for a woman from Queen's Village. Occasionally, she glanced at the letter, wanting to open it, but she was an American wife now and they were "cool" about these things. No suspicions. A marriage was a friendship in America, not a spy operation. Miles Davis played "My Funny Valentine" over and over, at the mercy of the rewind button, until 6 P.M.

"Here," she said, handing Nader the letter. She made no other acknowledgment, just left him alone with it and went into the kitchen to heat up yesterday's leftover spaghetti. Mrs. Donato's recipe, which Nader loved. He came in as she was setting the table. The letter was not in his hands; she made a mental note to check the wastebasket later. "Anything interesting?" she asked.

"No, just an old friend who wanted to say hello." His voice was steady and casual and he kissed her cheek with his usual lingering sweetness. He even lit a candle and placed it on the table between them as they ate. It was only his incessant foot-wiggling under the table that confirmed Siham's suspicion. When she couldn't find the letter the next morning, either in the wastebasket or in his pants pocket, she decided to visit Chestnut Street.

It took her forty minutes of brisk walking, and she realized that she'd worn bad shoes for such exercise. She also noticed, as city blocks streamed slowly by her, that the sidewalks were strewn with much less litter than in the Italian Market. The bricks of each building front were cleaner, and each door frame had a fresh coat of paint. Windows opened to little plants on their sills. The storefronts became fancier, as did the names. Gone were places called "Mike's Deli" and "Geno's Steaks." Here, there were salons, cafés, and food markets that advertised themselves as "gourmet." The sidewalks were red brick, not tan cement blocks separated by tufts of grass trying to break through. The men on these streets wore dark suits, not blue work uniforms, and the women got thinner with each block.

She approached 1012 Chestnut Street, a three-story house that was attached to the other homes on the block. A "town house," as Nader called them, like their own "row home," although they looked the same to her. At first she had a difficult time understanding this concept of homes attached like the links on a chain, a house where even your walls weren't entirely your own. When Nader had shown her the front of their building for the first time, she'd been delighted.

A puzzled Nader had asked, "You really like it?"

"Of course!" she'd answered, pointing to Washington Avenue on her left and Federal Street on her right. "This whole building is yours—you must have been right about America! You really can do well here." He'd laughed for several minutes before explaining that only the top two floors of the single unit in front of them was theirs. "It'll be a few years before we own a big house, but it'll happen in time," he'd said.

But 1012 Chestnut was nothing like their tiny apartment above the flower shop. Its white front steps, edged by a beautifully-carved stone rail, descended elegantly to the sidewalk. The door, made of dark wood, featured a round, brass knocker in its center, like an eye.

Like the Evil Eye painted on her blue stones. She stared up at the windows, awed and suddenly sad. A glimpse of a blonde head looking out of the second-story window sent her walking back. She hummed "My Funny Valentine" all the way home to calm the frenzied beat of her heart, and spent the rest of the day studying her verbs.

I hide. You hide. He/she/it hides.

I lie. We lie. They lie.

I cry. You cry. He/she/it cries.

I cry.

Their one-year anniversary was December 3rd, three weeks before Christmas. Nader had carefully planned a surprise, which included an early dinner at a Lebanese restaurant on South Street (where Siham was impressed to see that most of the clientele were not Arabs but Americans) and a concert in Atlantic City. The headliner was one of Siham's favorite Arab singers, who rarely performed in Palestine. Her sister Nadia would get a long letter about this.

As they drove to Atlantic City in their two-door Nissan, Nader explained that many Arab singers held concerts in the States. "When I was single, I would go to a concert, when I could afford it, with some Egyptian guys I worked with," he said. "We always hoped that we'd be attending these affairs with wives on our arms one day. I imagined taking my dream girl out for a romantic dinner, how she looked, how she spoke. And then I saw her outsmarting a leather vendor in the bazaar in Jerusalem!" They laughed and he reached for her hand in the darkness. He kissed the tips of her fingers gently, then lingered on her palm. "I'm so happy."

"Me, too." She truly was. She was also relieved that she had not refused his proposal. It was a risk, to marry a man who had spent so much time in America, but a lot of girls in Palestine did it. To get out of the country, to try their lives and their luck across the ocean, they married. One-month, even one-week engagements were not unusual, but Siham had never imagined she'd do it. How could you know about a man's past?, she used to argue. Unlike Jerusalem, where gossip lines kept everyone updated on their neighbors, someone could hide an entire life, conceal so many secrets behind America's veil. Even though Nader's family was originally from Jerusalem and had been sufficiently "checked out" by the al-Medanis, how could she trust him immediately? She had always claimed that she would get to know her fiancé for a long time, at least three years, before they married. Well, she was simply doing the "getting to know" part after the wedding.

"We're so lucky to have each other, Nader," she said, turning to look at his face, highlighted in short intervals by the lights along the expressway.

He kept the wheel steady with his left hand and wove the fingers of his right hand through hers. "When we first met, you *hated* me. I know you did. I thought you'd never agree to marry me, but I had to try."

"So you charmed my family to death? Good strategy."

He took his hand away to switch lanes then surrendered it again. "I just wanted you to like me so badly. If that meant flowers for your mother and American whiskey for your father and uncles . . ."

"And candy and chocolates for my sister, and perfume for my aunts," she continued. "That's what really got me. One day, Nadia walked into my room with chocolate all over her mouth and told me I had to marry you—or else she would!"

"Really?"

"Yes." Siham smiled to herself. All she'd heard from her mother was that a man was coming to the house to meet her, with the intention of eventual marriage. *He was an* Amerkani, *she'd said to her confused and bewildered daughter, but his roots were Arab. Siham had immediately suspected the brazen Linen Blazer from the bazaar last week and, sure enough, he strode into their living room the next evening, his arms laden with gifts, hair freshly combed, the same linen blazer crisply ironed. He told jokes, did impressions of celebrities, and casually worked in a discussion of the importance of family. He engaged her directly in conversation and seemed thrilled that she could hold her own when it came to culture and politics.*

After Nader left, her father called her into the kitchen and asked her opinion of this tall, dark, smooth-faced Arab from America. "You would have to live in America with him," her father had warned her. "In a city called Philadeelpheea." One month later, he walked her down the aisle of the Greek Orthodox church.

Now, six months later, she was beside him, on the way to a concert at the seashore. She would make sure this marriage lasted forever. Lasted happily. She clutched his hand even tighter, twisting her fingers between his in the way that she'd seen Carla twist the necks of the lilies.

Carla came up to the apartment one Thursday morning, two weeks later. It was almost Christmas and Siham had all the windows open, trying to infuse the rooms with fresh, cold air before she began to decorate. She had two red stockings on which she planned to embroider their names. She'd considered writing in glitter, but glitter would eventually wear off. Thread would imprint itself forever. She and Nader had bought a tree last night and she had yards of silver garland that she couldn't wait to use.

"It's like a freezer up here," Carla grunted, rubbing her arms. "I brought you two more orders for pillowcases, both black cloth, and this." She handed her $140. "From the last batch."

"Thank you, Carla." Siham rolled the wad of twenties and put them into the pocket of her cardigan. She purposefully didn't count them, knowing that Carla would pick up on it, her eyes flashing. She had such a temper, this one, so unlike her mother, whose smile was all gentle curves. A patient smile. She had probably learned to develop it over the years.

"Carla, I am making tea. Would you like a cup?" She could also be patient and kind. Why not? She was feeling good.

"Yes," Carla said, seeming startled, probably because Siham had never invited her to stay unless her mother was also there.

"Please sit." Siham indicated the large, green sofa in the living room and went to the kitchen. She poured two cups, set them on the tray with the sugarbowl and came out to find Carla standing underneath the wedding picture on the wall.

"Your dress is beautiful," Carla said. "Very traditional, with that full skirt and the long train. Very . . . well, bridal."

Siham gazed up at the portrait. She and Nader stood before the white stone wall that formed the back of her parent's house in Jerusalem. The Dome of the Rock, with its golden cupola, was visible in the background. Her own face looked pale, washed out by the whiteness of her dress, but Nader's olive skin blazed like the sun. Black brows that could look fierce when he was tired or irritated, but always masculine. She only had to smooth them with her index finger to reveal their gentleness. They framed large, caramel eyes that were always soft, that had emanated only love for the last three days, when she told him that she was pregnant.

"You know, I almost got married," Carla said, stirring lemon into her tea and perching on the edge of the sofa. "I had a fiancé years ago. An Irish guy from Northeast Philly."

Siham noted the way that Carla's hair curled softly at her neck. How her hands were slender and her fingers long, how her cheekbones sat high up in her face. Yes, a man *could* have loved her once.

"He worked at a dry cleaning and tailoring shop with his parents. When we got married, his parents said they were gonna retire. They were old, you know. John was their youngest of eight kids. They wanted us to take over the store, because I knew how to sew and handle customers."

"What happened for him?" Siham asked, making a mental note to look up the word "retire" later.

"He cheated on me. Knocked up another girl from his neighborhood."

"Knocked up?" Siham imagined him rapping his white knuckles against the forehead of some poor girl.

"Pregnant. He got her pregnant." Carla drained the last of her tea. "I refused to marry him after that. But I never married anyone else. Obviously." She smirked, closing the softness that had been subtly creeping into her face. "My mother said I'm just stubborn, that

I didn't want to give anyone else a chance. But that's my decision, I said, right?"

"Yes, of course. I am sorry for this happening to you."

"I'm not." Carla stood to leave. "Just proves you can't really trust men." She arched a painted eyebrow meaningfully in the direction of the wedding portrait. "Thanks for the tea." Her dark eyes glittered and Siham felt nauseous.

Later that night, when Nader was snoring softly, Siham rummaged through her wooden storage chest until she found what she wanted. She crept downstairs to the living room and taped a small, blue bead, painted with the Eye, to the back of the portrait. She also put a small one in the nursery, next to the door, above the shelf where the Barbie army sat patiently in line, waiting for a child's hands to animate them. She would have to find another, a larger one, to replace the one above her bed. How could she have left that precious space unprotected for so long? She climbed back into the bed, shivering.

She had seen the Evil Eye itself today, sipping tea on her sofa.

It was not enough. The Eye worked its evil the very next day, assuming the shape, not of a black-haired, meddlesome spinster, but of a tall, slim blonde woman. Powder-blue suit, big shoulder pads, collarless jacket with a scalloped neck. Siham didn't understand why she focused on this detail, but she did. Maybe she'd known already, from the moment she heard Mrs. Donato's voice calling her down, she'd known it would be this woman with hard, rounded calves and pale brows. Sitting calmly in a chair in the flower shop, looking like Attorney Barbie.

"Hi," she said, standing up. She was tall, too, which made Siham feel even smaller. "Are you Nader's wife?"

"Yes. My name is Siham al-Jundi." Thank God she'd at least had the foresight to put on lipstick and pull a comb through her hair. She suddenly felt that it mattered. "Can I help you?"

"I need to get in touch with Nader, to collect some money he owes me. I've tried to reach him several times, but it seems like he's avoiding me and I can't wait any longer."

"Money? For what?"

"Well, that's really between Nader and myself," replied Attorney Barbie, her voice brusque and dismissive. "When do you expect him home?"

"Maybe in one hour." Siham was acutely aware of Carla's glittering, inquisitive eyes staring at them from behind the counter. She felt even more minuscule and tiny next to this living doll, this American dream.

"I will return then. Please tell him to expect me." She slung her purse over her shoulder and headed for the door.

"What shall I tell him your name is?" called Siham after her.

With a weary sigh, as if it hurt to speak, she said, "Just tell him that his first wife came by to see him."

Siham refused to allow Nader to bring Homewrecker Barbie upstairs to the apartment. "Talk with her down there," she said when Mrs. Donato's voice summoned him. Nader squeezed her hand apologetically and descended to the flower shop.

All the while that he was downstairs, she could only think furiously that he had brought the evil into their home. With his lies, his guilt. He had explained it, of course. He had even cried with her a little. After he'd graduated from the university, they were going to deport him, he said. He'd needed a green card. So he got married, like a business deal. She'd done him a favor, but he still owed her two thousand dollars that he didn't have.

But had they been lovers? No, he insisted, so adamantly that she believed him. "She wouldn't have an Arab in her bed. Just in her third-story room, for the promise of six thousand dollars," he said. The third story of the house on Chestnut Street, in case the INS checked up on them. He'd even paid her rent during those three years, in addition to the money she wanted. Two months after their official divorce, he'd returned to the Old Country and spent the remaining two thousand dollars on his wedding. His "real and meaningful" wedding, not the sham one of almost four years ago.

Siham sat at the window in her embroidery room, looking down at the sidewalk below. She had $850 in an envelope, tucked beneath layers of fabric and spools of thread in her craft box. She'd wanted to use it to buy a new crib, a changing table, and a rocking chair to put in this room. This room would soon be a nursery. If the baby was a girl, as she hoped, she had planned to buy the beautiful set of baby furniture she'd seen in the Sunday circular, an ashy wood with brass details on the drawer handles.

A blonde head appeared below and turned right heading down 9th Street, probably toward her beautiful and elegant home with its plants on the windowsill and clean, swept sidewalks. She was abandoning the numbered streets for one with an elegant and thoroughly American name: Chestnut. Only Americans named their streets after trees, instead of after presidents and wars and prophets. She probably wouldn't even walk; she'd hail a cab along the way or maybe get into her expensive car.

Nader would come upstairs now, probably with a rose Mrs. Donato would wisely press into his hands. He would be climbing the steps, hoping it would make her smile. And she would smile, as genuinely as she could stretch her lips, and say that she understood. That it would take a while to forget it, but that they had to think about the baby now. Then she would hand him the envelope with the money and ask him to never mention this again. She would not tell him about the nursery set, just quietly toss out the picture in the circular.

And she would write her mother, asking her to mail a few more blue stones. She had to be more careful from now on.

Survivor

I walked slowly, carefully, along the sidewalk, avoiding the icy patches. Aliyah held my arm with her hands, strong and secure. We were headed to 5th and South Streets, to the used bookstore at that intersection, where Aliyah wanted to buy the new novel by her favorite Indian-American author.

"It just came out a few weeks ago," she chattered as we crept at an excruciating pace, "so for sure someone's read it by now and sold it to the bookstore. I can't wait to read it myself, because I loved her first book—the short stories. I loaned it to you, right? Did you ever read it?"

"Nope," I said. "I didn't get a chance to read too much, even though I guess I had tons of time on my hands."

"That's OK . . . you were recovering, and that was the most important thing."

I noticed that she didn't say, "You're still recovering," which is what was factually true. She implied that I had recovered, that my recovery was in the past, some obstacle that had been surmounted. Somehow, even though I knew it wasn't true, I felt a little better.

Funny. I'd grown up with Aliyah; Hanan, and Reema, and I'd always thought Aliyah, petite and slim, was the weakest of us all. Physically, for sure, but emotionally too. She was a writer, and she usually joked that that was why she was so sensitive. I always imagined that any sort of tragedy—heartbreak, death, illness—would destroy her, send her into a decades-long funk in which she would pine away in her room, writing into a journal or composing angry and depressed poetry. Maybe I didn't understand her as well as I thought. Maybe I didn't understand any of my friends. And maybe they didn't understand me either.

"Remember when we were kids," I suddenly said, realizing as soon as I spoke that I'd interrupted Aliyah's chattering and had changed the subject completely.

She didn't seem to mind, just looked over at me. "What's that?"

"Remember when we were kids," I started again, "and we said that when we grew up, we would all buy a big house and move in together?"

"Yep . . . and the house was going to have seven different rooms, each one a different color of the rainbow."

"Mine was going to be the red one."

"And mine the purple. I think Reema took the yellow room and Hanan took the blue one."

"I think we had to convince her to take the blue one. She originally wanted brown or black or something like that," I reminded Aliyah. I couldn't believe I remembered all these details, but the image was clearly in my mind. We were about ten years old, sitting in Reema's parents' house on Tasker Street, in the basement where the TV and the dollhouse were. We'd even drawn sketches of what the house would look like, and since each of us wanted a turret, the house had four, one in each corner.

"Yeah, I guess Hanan had a dismal outlook back then," Aliyah said, laughing. "In some ways, she still does, but I guess I would be the same if I'd gone through what she did."

We reached the bookstore and thankfully entered its warm, welcoming atmosphere. The only other customers were a young couple standing by the mystery books section. Aliyah headed to the back, right section, while I grabbed the first book my hand touched on the shelf and sat down on one of the overstuffed, worn-down couches. One of the owner's cats leapt out from beneath it, startling me.

"Sorry 'bout that," the owner, a plump, bald man behind the counter said.

"No problem," I said, waving my hand as if to dismiss it. I couldn't remember his name, but Hanan and Aliyah knew him well, since they came in often. At least, Hanan used to, when she lived in the area. When she moved to University City after the wedding, she didn't come down to South Philly except to visit one of us or her father.

Aliyah sauntered by me, waving a copy of the novel, as she headed for the counter. She paid for it—$11 for the hardcover—and plopped down beside me on the couch with her treasure. She flipped through the pages quickly and then began reading the inside flaps and the back cover.

I asked her about Hanan. "I hardly ever see her."

"She's just busy with Michael. And now she has her baskets selling in this gift shop on Walnut Street."

"Ooohhhh . . ." I said, smirking.

Aliyah laughed. "Hanan and I are still South Philly at heart, don't worry."

"Are her baskets doing well?"

"They're actually selling. The lady who owns the place sold eight baskets last week, and five so far this week. Each one sells for about $30, and Hanan keeps 80 percent of it."

"So if she sells eight a week," I said, quickly calculating the numbers in my head, "that's almost $200 a week that she keeps, profit."

"How do you do that?" Aliyah asked, shaking her head. "I can barely add single digits without using my fingers."

"I'm glad she's doing well," I continued. "She was good at crafts and stuff, even when we were little. She used to help us all with our projects."

"Yep, and she learned all that stuff from her mother—embroidery, weaving, all that stuff. My mother never taught me that. I don't think she even knows how to do it."

"I'm glad she's making a little money on the side. That'll help her a bit."

"George actually bought one of her baskets," Aliyah said, then stopped, looking awkwardly up at me. "He was being supportive."

"That's great. I have no problem with that."

She looked down at her book, and we sat quietly reading for a while. The book I'd picked up was Isabel Allende's *Paula*. I leafed through it, skimming the first two pages, but decided that I really didn't want to read anything that would depress me. Reading my medical reports had depressed me enough.

I glanced at Aliyah, who was intently reading the first chapter. Aliyah had already had one heartbreak. She'd traveled to Jerusalem for a summer and reunited with a family friend there. I remember getting emails from her, emails she'd sent to me, Reema, and Hanan on a regular basis, updating us on her adventures. The guy had proven to be committed, charming, but they had a lot of issues nonetheless.

"It's not that he thinks I should be 100 percent Arabic," she'd said in one of her emails, "but he said he wants me to be less American. Whatever that means, right?"

And that was the problem, I knew. It was the same problem—the same sense of being uncomfortable—that I felt now with George. Of course, I was the one who had ended it, so I had no right to feel regret.

George first arrived in a dream one night, the way my grandmother used to. She appeared regularly, calming my fears and giving me advice about everything from upcoming exams to witnessing one of Mama's crying jags. "Your mother is lonely," she would explain to me soothingly, "and she just needs to release her stress. Let her do what she needs to do."

For a long time, I didn't tell anyone about those dreams, those midnight conversations with my grandmother. I wasn't afraid that I'd be called crazy. Not at all. It was more like a cherished secret that I didn't want to ruin by exposure.

And then when I was twenty-two, George appeared in a dream as well. Except that I didn't know who he was, because I hadn't actually met him yet. The circumstances that prompted the dream were still clear in my mind.

I had spent the summer after college graduation interviewing for jobs. Not everyone was eager to hire a business major, fresh out of college, and everyone was looking for experience, experience, experience. How was I to get experience, I complained to my mother and my friends, when nobody would give me a job?

By July I was hunting for internships. I could intern for a while, and continue looking for work in the meantime, so that even if I didn't have a lot of experience, I could still say, "Well, I'm currently interning at . . ."

I came home one evening, after a long day: three interviews in a row, all in different parts of the city. Mama had made my favorite meal—*malfoof*, with steamed cabbage leaves. I tossed my briefcase onto the sofa, and plopped myself down at the kitchen table. "Mama, bless your hands," I said. "This really looks good."

She kissed my cheek, then sliced up two lemons. My favorite thing was to squeeze some juice on the rolled cabbage leaves, which would seep into the roll of rice and meat encased within each one, giving it a tart flavor.

"Good, *habibti*. I'm sorry you had a rough day."

"Thanks . . . we'll see what happens."

We continued the meal in a pleasant silence. Later, as I washed the dishes, I suddenly had a horrible realization. I threw down the dish towel and hurried into the living room, where Mama sat embroidering a new pillow and watching the evening news.

"I feel like an idiot."

"Why?" she asked, looking up, startled.

"I was just thinking that the last time you made *malfoof* was a year ago, and then it hit me that you only make it once a year on the day . . . for Baba."

"It's OK, Nadia *habibti.*"

"I was so busy the last few weeks, I guess it slipped my mind."

I kissed her on the cheek, and she patted my face, then returned quietly to her embroidery.

I resumed my dishwashing, letting the hot water soak and wrinkle my fingertips. *Malfoof* had been Baba's favorite meal as well, and it had been the last meal she'd made for him before he died. It was so long ago, but she still marked the anniversary of his death by making that meal.

I wish I'd known my father better than I had. I have only scattered memories—his mustached smile; the slim, gold crucifix he wore around his neck, nestled in the black hairs that curled up on his chest; the mole behind his neck that I used to look at when he gave me rides on his back; the neatly trimmed hairline behind his ears; the slam of the door and the burst of sound, because his habit was to start talking about his day the minute he walked into the apartment, whether or not he saw my mother in front of him. He just assumed she would be there, standing by the stove or playing with me, ready to listen, waiting for the sound of his footsteps on the stairs.

The hot water became almost scalding, and I quickly pulled my hands out of the stream. Mama had also assumed that he would be there, always coming home at the same time, carrying a treat for me or a little gift for her, always pulling her into his arms and saying, "Your hair smells *so* good."

It only lasted a short time, but Mama lived on those memories, and she planned to live on them the rest of her life. Could it be possible to find a love that could sustain you for that long, even after the person you loved was gone? Did that kind of love even exist anymore? I wondered if I would ever find someone like that. "Probably not," I thought to myself, peering into the living room at Mama, still stitching away, watching but not really listening to the news. Soon she would fall asleep, and I would prod her awake and then she'd tread softly into her room and collapse into her queen-sized bed. And it would be a night like every other night—slow, content, simple.

I finished washing the dishes and put them away, then spent the rest of the evening in the kitchen, reviewing my resume and reading the want ads in the *Philadelphia Inquirer*.

It was not that night that George arrived in my dream. It was at least two nights later, because it was the same night that I finally landed an internship. Brookes, Inc., had called me in for a second interview and offered me a two-month paid internship, in which I would be assisting one of their ad executives. I would get $3000 a month, and the internship would possibly lead to a job, they told me. "We usually give these internships to people still in school, but we made an exception in this case. The owner thinks you have a lot of promise," the hiring officer told me as I sat in her office after the interview, filling out the paperwork.

Mama and I celebrated by walking down to Pat's and gorging on cheesesteaks, something I loved to do but she rarely did. She didn't like to eat out in general, but this was a special occasion. We sat on the orange plastic tables on the sidewalk outside of Pat's.

I loved to look at the photographs of celebrities—all of whom had eaten at Pat's at some point—lined along the glass windows. Mama enjoyed watching the kids in the park across the street play basketball, showing off for one another and for passersby. Mama gingerly ate her steak in a ladylike way, while I devoured mine. When we returned home, I called Aliyah, Reema, and Hanan and told them the good news before collapsing into bed.

I drifted for a time, then was pulled into a dream. I found myself sitting on a red floor pillow in the middle of a large room with marble tiles. This is where I usually waited for my grandmother to show up. But this time, she never came . . . instead, as I waited, a door opened in the far corner, behind me. I turned to look, and the figure of a tall man approached me. As he got closer and closer, I could see that he was very handsome, with black hair, olive skin, a smooth face. He sat beside me—the red, embroidered pillow suddenly became big

39

enough to accommodate us both—held my hand and asked my name.

"Nadia."

"Then you're the one I've been looking for," he said happily. We sat that way for a long time, just quietly holding hands—no embarrassment, no hesitation, nothing awkward. He never told me his name, and I did not ask. I knew who he was, on a deeper level than name recognition. I recognized him as a part of myself.

The St. Agnes Hospital on Broad Street felt like a nightclub—nurses and aides running around, chatting and laughing, all wearing bright pink and coral lipsticks, hair lifted high and decorously, like a South Philly Eiffel Tower. I immediately sensed that, in my gray pinstriped pantsuit, I was out of place. And yet, fifteen years ago, when Mama and I had been summoned here to see Baba, these nurses had taken me in their arms.

Mama had refused to let me go in the recovery room to see Baba immediately after the surgery. The doctor's face was grim, and that was when Mama turned to Hanan's and Aliyah's fathers and said, "Keep her here."

"Noooooo!" I'd screamed, darting toward the double doors into which she'd slipped. But they each grabbed one of my arms and held me back.

"*La, habibti . . . la, ya* Nadia." They tried to comfort me, but I was inconsolable, scared because something was wrong with Baba and nobody was telling me.

That's when one of the nurses approached me—I remember she had a huge chest, like two cannon balls, a small waist, and short legs. Her lipstick was a baby pink, her bleached blonde hair piled on top of her head, her eyeshadow a pasty, matte blue.

"Come with me, hon," she said, taking my hand and pulling me gently toward the nurses' station. She took me behind the counter, and I followed numbly, though curiously.

"Look what we have here," she said, pointing to a small drawer behind the counter. Two other nurses, both middle-aged like my nurse, sat there, grinning at me. "Go ahead and open it, sweetie," one of them urged.

I pulled open the drawer and found a treasure chest of candy—Twizzlers, Baby Ruth bars, bags of red Swedish fish, and lollipops.

"Take some with you, hon," my nurse said. "We don't like to see anyone sad here."

Hours later, when Mama told me that Baba had died, that he had not survived the accident or the surgery, I forgot all about those nurses and the drawer full of Twizzlers. But for that small space of time, I had been content, quiet.

Now I stood here in a different capacity, an intern with Brookes, Inc., to meet with some doctors and chief executives about their ad campaign. I was with six other representatives of the company, and I had been told that all I needed to do was keep quiet and take notes.

One of the nurses, looking coolly at our suits and polished shoes, directed us to the second floor, to the executive offices, and from there we were ushered into a large boardroom with a long wooden table. I sat at the end, hoping to stay as inconspicuous as possible.

Ten minutes later, the representatives of the hospital strode in—about twelve people in all, some wearing suits and some sporting white coats. We were introduced to the vice president of the hospital, to the director of public relations, to several of the head doctors, as well as to some staff members and some medical residents.

My eyes stayed focused on one medical resident, wearing a nametag that said "George Haddad, M.D." He had to be Arabic, by his name and by his looks. His shiny black hair was combed back from his face, and his large brown eyes looked like pools of liquid chocolate. He sat opposite me, at the end of the table, and smiled.

I do not remember taking notes, but when I got back to my office, I saw that I had filled a legal pad with squiggles and letters that meant almost nothing to me. All I could remember was that, during a break in the meeting, right after our Brookes team had presented a video of our campaign idea, George walked right over to me and shook my hand again.

"I'm George Haddad. Your name was Nadia?"

"Yes, Nadia al-Jundi."

"Nadia . . ." His voice had a gentle accent, unmistakably Arabic but not as heavy or as pronounced as that of my mother. "You are Arab."

"Yes. Palestinian."

"*Bit-kalami Araby?*" he asked me.

"*Na'am,*" I answered him. Yes, I did speak Arabic. And I would speak any language he wanted me to at that moment.

After the meeting, he asked if I would like to have coffee with him sometime. "I am new in Philadelphia. Just doing my residency here, and I don't really know anyone. You're the first Arab person I have met so far."

We met at the Melitta Café on South Street the following day. I arrived earlier that he did—later I would learn that George, in a typically Arab way, was always running late—and waited at a table at the end of the shop, tucked away in a corner. A waitress brought me a small cappuccino, and I told her I was expecting someone.

"I'll come back when your friend gets here then," she said cheerily.

Fifteen minutes later she returned, followed by George.

"Yes," he said to the waitress, not taking his eyes off me, "she's the one I've been looking for."

After the accident, I started reading Frida Kahlo's work. About when she was a young woman, riding the trolley when it was involved in a horrible accident. A rod from the trolley broke loose and impaled her abdomen.

This is not what happened to me. My accident was not nearly so dramatic. But I will never forget my mother's face when the doctor told us quietly, "The uterus was ruptured. We managed to save most of it, but it is also damaged internally."

A hysterosalpingogram, performed a few days later, confirmed the worst: the doctor pushed a dark ink up through my cervix and into my uterus, while Mama and I watched it on the X-Ray monitor. The ink crept up through my cervix, but then did not fill out the shape of my uterus, pooling instead into several disparate and jagged pockets. "Those are bands of scar tissue," the doctor explained. "They formed in response to the trauma."

"Can you remove them?" my mother asked, her voice surprisingly calm. I twisted my head around to peer up at her. She was watching the monitor with wide eyes, not blinking.

"We could, but it's very likely that they will grow back."

"What about children?" Mama asked. This time, her voice sounded terrified.

"I doubt she would be able to carry a fetus to full-term," the doctor said directly. I almost appreciated his bluntness. "I don't even think an embryo would be able to implant itself in the uterine wall, because of the scar tissue that is in the way and which has probably compromised the quality of the lining."

When they had wheeled me back into my room, and the nurse was checking my IV, Mama excused herself and stepped into the small, adjoining bathroom. She did not come out for several minutes and, when she did, her eyes were raw and red.

I started to say something, to comfort her, to tell her it was OK and that I was not upset by what the doctor had said, but just then George walked in, carrying flowers.

"Hi, *ameera*," he said, with a broad smile. He kissed my mother's cheek and then came over, bent down and kissed mine. "Are they taking care of you the way they should be?" he asked, professionally glancing over the chart at the foot of my bed.

"I think the nurse wanted that," Mama said, snatching the chart from his hands and heading toward the door. "I'll bring it to her."

And I understood: I should not tell George what had happened. I could read my mother's thoughts as though a bubble had formed above her head to dictate them to me.

Several days later, once the shock of the doctor's diagnosis had settled in, she explained it to me. "*Habibti*, George is the only son in his family—he has four sisters. His parents will definitely want him to have many children so he can carry on the family name." She had pulled a chair up next to my bed, and sat beside me, mindlessly rubbing my fingernails with the pads of her own fingers.

"I see."

"They will not accept it if they know that you might have trouble having children. And that will put George in a very bad situation."

"So should I tell him?"

"I don't know."

"He doesn't care about that kind of thing, Mama. He always said he would like to adopt other kids someday. He worked in the camps, remember? He has a big heart. Plus," I reminded her, "he was the one who caused the accident. Even Hanan and John said it—he wasn't paying attention. He missed the stop sign."

Mama was choosing her words carefully, I could tell. "Maybe George would not care, but his parents will care. They will want a child who is their own blood, of their own genes. And they will force George—pull him away from you."

"We don't even know them, Mama." I knew she was right, but I was trying to think of as many logical arguments as I could.

"We don't have to know them, *habibti*. They are an Arab family, with only one son, who have put all their savings to send him to medical school in America. Do you think they will accept for him to marry and not have children?"

Part of me raged against her words, and against her. It seemed for some reason that she was more concerned about George's happiness than mine.

"Sometimes we have to put our happiness aside for the sake of the ones we love." She said it simply, directly, looking right in my eyes, and I suddenly began weeping wildly—hating myself for ever doubting her and hating George for putting me in this position in the first place.

I did not return to work for six months, and even then Brookes allowed me to work mostly from home, going to the office just twice a week. On my first day back, they threw me a surprise party. My desk was decorated with pink and purple streamers, and silver-colored balloons had been tied to the back of my chair. My co-workers stood around my desk, clapping as I walked in, leaning heavily on my cane.

I only stayed a few hours that day, and left shortly after noon because I quickly became more tired than I thought I would. My boss nodded when I told him I wasn't feeling well, then rang for the tech people. "We need a laptop asap for one of our employees," he said crisply into the phone. "They'll be here in half an hour," he said as he hung up. "Stay until then."

They presented me with a laptop, copied all my files onto it, and equipped it with an email program. Several days later, they sent a technician to our apartment to install a high-speed Internet connection.

Mama couldn't stop telling the other mothers about it. She invited all the ladies to our apartment for their usual coffee chat. They came into my room to see me, where I was lying in bed and clicking away on the laptop. They each kissed my cheek, and brushed away my apologies for not getting up. "Rest, rest," Aliyah's mother said.

Later I heard them in the kitchen, speaking about me. "And her company gave her a computer for herself, to use from home and they even came to the house and did all the connections for her," Mama said.

Aliyah's, Reema's, and Hanan's mothers cooed their amazement.

"She's very important in her company, you know," my mother said matter-of-factly. I rolled my eyes. I'd only been with Brookes for less than a year, and my mother was painting me as the CEO.

"God keep her always for you," Hanan's mother said. "She's an excellent girl, your Nadia."

"We both have wonderful girls," my mother responded.

I stopped typing to listen for her response, but she hesitated.

"She *is*," my mother insisted. "Hanan has a good heart."

"She's a stubborn girl," Hanan's mother replied. "Her father is sick now, all the time, and she doesn't come to see him. Sometimes she comes, but only when she knows I will not be there." She paused. "What did I do to her—do I deserve this? Tell me, do I?" I pushed the laptop off my lap and sat up straighter, leaning toward the open door to hear their snatches of Arabic as best as I could.

"You're a wonderful mother," they soothed her. "We're all in the same position—we raise them the best we can in this country."

"Yes, I know! Me, who gave that girl all my energy and all my effort! If that Amerkani wanted to marry my daughter, he should enter my house from the front door and not the back door!"

"Good for you!"

"You have a clever tongue, *ya* Layla."

When they left, they all filed into the bedroom again to say goodbye, to kiss me again, and to wish me a speedy recovery. "Soon we will see you walk down the aisle, *insh'allah*," said Reema's mother. I knew she meant George—everyone knew about me and George— and I knew she was sincere, but I felt like she had punched me in the stomach. I tried to speak, but couldn't say anything intelligible, and my mother swooped in to rescue me. "*Insh'allah*, we will also see Reema doing the same," she said, and everyone smiled and everyone was happy.

Except for me. While Mama escorted them to the door, I looked at the blue beads she had taped to the foot of my bed. My mother believed in the Evil Eye strongly—she blamed it for Baba's death still— and she had blue beads all over the house: in drawers, above the kitchen table, on the living room wall. The beads were flat, round, made of glass. A deep blue, "the color of the Mediterranean," Mama said, with a black center representing the pupil of the eye.

I saw the beads, and I was reminded that I was a survivor, like my mother.

ALIYAH

Aliyah's Fan

Many years ago, Aliyah's father had given her five dollars for winning the fourth-grade essay contest. More importantly, he had finally allowed her to have her own room—the beautifully decorated, pristinely maintained, but rarely occupied guest bedroom facing the alley, which flowed like a concrete river between the cemented backyards of the row houses on the block. Despite its paltry 10' by 10' size— some people's closets were bigger—it was finally hers. Her brothers had resented her for months and plotted revenge from their bunk-bed headquarters in the middle room, but it was her space now, this room with a window and salmon pink walls and a picture of the Virgin Mary, wearing bright blue robes, that hung above her bed. And the door even had a working lock.

This first memory of her modest success seeped into Aliyah's thoughts as she closed her apartment's door behind her, listened for the "click," and headed to the subway station. Having been summoned by a late-night phone call, she was going to visit her parents. "Your story, in that magazine," her mother had said. "We just want to ask you about it."

Then, in an urgent whisper, "*Abuki za'laan.*" She'd heard it before, though usually in reference to something her brothers had done: "Your father is furious."

As she briskly covered the three blocks to the station, Aliyah imagined him sitting in the kitchen last night, reading her story while he sipped her mother's tea: Lipton infused with fresh peppermint leaves. Every Arab mother grew peppermint in her garden or, in her mother's case, in the pot on the ledge of the kitchen window. He'd read, often flipping back to the front cover of the magazine to see again, "Featuring fiction by . . . and Aliyah al-Rawi." He'd smile to himself and think, "Goddamn it, my daughter is a *real* writer." ("Real" meant, of course, that she was getting paid for her words, not merely in the contributor's copies that were like jewels to her but that her father disdained.) But then, he would arrive at the part in the middle, the part she had rewritten, cut, reinserted, and reworked a dozen times. One paragraph, eighty-five words, caused his eyebrows to arch and his fingers to pull agitatedly at the ends of his Hercule Poirot mustache. And he would think, "Goddamn it, I can't believe she wrote this!"

When she jogged down the steps into the station, the familiar stench of heat and urine rose up to welcome her, and she reminded herself that she'd *had* to include that part. It had been too funny, too perfect to slice out. The words slipped back into her mind one by one, as if to parallel the clink her tokens made as she dropped them into the machine. "*Uncle Ghassan's blue beret looked painfully snug on his rather large head and the stench of J&B on his breath alerted the bride. He gave his nephew's new wife a sleepy smile. As he leaned in to kiss her cheek in congratulations, he started—to everyone's horror—to tip over in the direction of the white-clad queen of the day. His hand snatched at anything—and settled on the pearl-sewn bodice of her dress, ripping it down to her waist as he fell.*" Even now, as she boarded the train, Aliyah smiled to herself. No free seats, so she stood by the door and wrapped her hand around a slim, aluminum pole as the train jerked forward. That wedding scene had been born of her editing adventure, mainly because she had abandoned all efforts to disguise the truth. After all, she was hardly the first writer to recycle real life.

A sign plastered to the train wall read: "Keep Philadelphia beautiful." A picture of a teenager tossing crumbled paper into a trash can illustrated the point. Aliyah immediately looked at the reality of empty soda cans and Tastykake wrappers underneath the seats and at the mosaic of flattened, hardened gum balls that decorated the plastic armrests and brown floors.

She stepped out of the station onto Broad Street. In Center City, where horse-drawn carriages paraded tourists around cultural sights and City Hall, Broad Street was known as the Avenue of the Arts. Here, in South Philadelphia, it was just Broad Street. She walked past St. Agnes Hospital, at the intersection of Broad and Passyunk. She'd been born here twenty-nine years ago, the year that Pablo Neruda took the Nobel. "I'm going to win it too," she had announced at the dinner table at the age of twelve. Her father came home a week later with an almost-new Sears typewriter.

"From the pawn shop on 6th and South," he'd said proudly. "No case, and the hyphen key is missing, but it still works real good."

"Baba, how come I don't get one?" her brother whined, looking sullen.

"Because Aliyah needs it to write." Interesting verb choice, she'd thought. *Needs.*

Aliyah's mother opened the door to their red brick row house and smiled wanly. "Hi, *habibti.*"

She looked tired, Aliyah thought, kissing her cheek. Her mother was tall and lean, with the blue-green eyes prized by Arab men that Aliyah had always regretted not inheriting. Instead, she resembled her father, with dusky skin and small, dark brown eyes. She stepped inside, to the living room with the books and magazines strewn over the glass coffee table, the silk flowers arranged in vases tucked in every available space. Her father's *oud* leaning its long neck against the corduroy ottoman. She plopped down on the familiar, plastic-covered couch. "When are you ever going to take this stuff off?" she asked teasingly. The blue, French-style furniture had been sheathed in plastic since she had been a child. Only when guests came over—and, even then, only very old or important ones—was the plastic peeled off and the fabric permitted to breathe.

"It's the only way to keep them clean," her mother retorted, frowning and bending to the carpet. Taking a tissue out of her pocket, she swiped at a speck of brown dirt, which Aliyah had brought in on her shoes, near the front door.

"We're all grown up now," Aliyah teased. "You don't need to cover them anymore. And the plastic sticks to your legs in the summer. It's so uncomfortable."

"So, we can expect to read about them in your next story?" Her father's deep voice charged the atmosphere dramatically.

"Hi, Baba." She stood up and went to kiss his cheek, which he received coldly. She stepped back and studied his face. It was a face of lines—the line of his mustache, parallel to the line of his black brows, perpendicular to the line of his elegant, high-ridged nose. Perfect symmetry. "You're upset with me, Baba?"

"What do you think?" He stalked away, toward the kitchen.

"I made some lunch. Let's all sit down and eat," her mother said, ushering Aliyah into the kitchen as well. The table was spread with the traditional *mezzeh*: yogurt, cheese cubes, cucumber salad, hummus, and hot pita bread. Aliyah glanced furtively at her subdued father throughout the meal, while her mother spoke casually and nonchalantly about Uncle Moussa's new house in the suburbs and Cousin Deena's upcoming wedding. "It's costing your uncle $40,000—can you imagine?"

After he'd taken his last bite of hummus, swiveling his bread around the dish ("Clean your plates. Never waste food"—the mantra of her childhood), her father sat up straight, shoulders pulled back, and cleared his throat. He spoke and his voice was like the deepest chord of the *oud*. She remembered how he would pluck a string, let-ting it reverberate through the hollow, wooden body of the instru-ment. America's intolerance of accents and Palestine's intolerance of stability had destroyed any chance he'd had to become a famous mu-sician, singing the songs he composed and copied carefully into Aliyah's old composition notebooks, whose used pages he had simply ripped out: "Why buy new ones? These ones are fine." He'd become a grocery shopowner, trading the quaver of the *oud* for the healthy bang of a cash register, but Aliyah's best childhood memories were of waking up soon after dawn to the music of the lute wafting through the house.

"You are supposed to be a writer, no? And a writer uses her imagi-nation to *create* characters and . . . situations. Right or wrong?"

"Right."

"So where is your imagination in this story? You create nothing. You only take an embarrassing family story and tell it to the world, like those Home Funniest Videos."

"Funniest Home Videos."

"It does not matter. You do not even disguise your relatives—just a little mask, like a different name. How will your uncle feel? He didn't mean to ruin your cousin's wedding. He wishes that everyone will forget it. He doesn't even drink anymore. But now . . ."

"I doubt that he'll even read it, Baba."

"Of course he will." His fingers tugged anxiously at his mustache. "I gave almost everyone a copy of the magazine."

"Really?"

"We ordered twenty copies of it," her mother explained, standing up to collect the dirty dishes. "We even sent one to your grandfather back home."

"But he doesn't even read English," Aliyah protested.

"So?" her father muttered. "He'll be happy to show people your name on the cover. Soon, the whole village will know that his grand-daughter is a writer."

If only he knew what you were writing. It hung between them, un-spoken, suspended in the air like a raised fist.

She stood in her old bedroom, which looked unchanged despite the six-year vacancy. Lilac walls, the purple and white blanket on the bed, and then the only other piece of furniture that the tiny room could accommodate: her wooden desk, swiped from a garage sale for $5, stripped, sanded, and revarnished by her father over a series of Sunday afternoons. Its polished, unmarred surface shone like amber and Aliyah leaned over like Narcissus to scrutinize her blurry reflection. The day he had finished varnishing it, her father forbade her from carving her initials into the wood. "Don't junk it up," he'd said. "Leave it beautiful."

Aliyah opened the Venetian blinds and gazed down into the alley behind the house. In the early afternoon light, it did not seem so dingy, but rather like a labyrinthine tunnel that connected everyone's backyards in a chain of square, cement links.

"Aliyah, let's talk." Baba's deep voice came from behind her.

"I wasn't trying to embarrass you." Better to speak plainly and spare the drama. "I was only writing a good story. And people liked it."

"I did not."

"Well, guess what? The editor *did*. And he reads thousands of stories a year, but he liked mine." She snapped the blinds shut and faced him. "He liked the 'realistic details'."

"I hate to discourage you, and I know that is what I am doing." He sat on the bed. "I always encouraged you, right or wrong?"

"Right."

"But *I* have to answer to the family when they start asking questions and getting upset, not you."

Of course that was what it had come down to, the family and its dignity. She'd known that. "I'm sorry. Really."

"Could you not have written about *anything* else? You had to use your uncle's one moment of embarrassment. My God, he is my brother!"

"He's done things like that a million times, Baba. Why didn't the family get him some help sooner instead of worrying about a ten-page story?"

"It is not *your* story! It is his. Make up your own, for Christ's sake!"

The subway ride home was quiet, disturbed only by the usual shifting of the car as it hugged the bends in the track. An elderly black woman and an Asian teenaged girl spoke softly about the new mayor, shaking their heads, while a heavy Italian man with a thick mustache watched the screen of the Gameboy his young son was intensely playing. Aliyah swayed with the force that wracked her brain with a mix of guilt and righteousness. For the next few days, she couldn't write anything. Her apartment had never been so clean, her friends had never received so many chatty phone calls. Meanwhile, her pencils remained unsharpened, her legal tablet unscratched, her laptop unplugged.

One day, she finally boarded the subway and returned home to tell her father that all the stories in the world had to be hers, or else she would never find her own voice, never write from the heart.

Only her father's car was parked outside. Her mother was probably at her friend Reema's home, discussing her "stubborn husband" and her "inconsiderate daughter" while sipping coffee with Reema's mother. Better like this anyway. There was no answer to her knock, so she let herself in with her own key. She heard the strong chords of the *oud* coming from the direction of the kitchen, in the back of the house. An elbow peeked out from the kitchen doorway, and a chair slightly pulled out from the table. She imagined the rest of her father, sitting straight in the chair, picking out his frustration on the strings, transforming it into an exhausting, consuming loveliness.

She sank, trance-like, into the plastic-covered chair and absorbed the wordless song, the alternating and conflicting notes that formed a harmonious wave, gentle as it swept over her weariness. There would surely be raised voices, blistering words soon, but she hoped that he wouldn't realize her presence for at least a few more minutes, that he would continue on this wave, carrying her along.

Reading Coffee Cups

It all started when Nader, God rest his soul, bought his wife Siham a dishwasher. The other women in our circle were not pleased, but they kept quiet. I was unable to do that—it has always been one of my bad qualities.

"She only has one child," I told Layla, "and I have four. Could she possibly have more dishes to clean than I do?"

Layla shrugged, making no commitment. "I only have one child too, Imm Nabeel." I could have smacked myself, because of course she only had one—her daughter, Hanan, who strutted around the neighborhood like a boy. She wore tight, acid-washed jeans, carefully ripping out the knees, and made her hair stick up in the front. She sprayed it so much that it stood off her head like a peacock's feathers. Abu Nabeel joked that airplanes swerved to avoid crashing into it.

Aliyah always rolled her eyes when I spoke of Hanan, because those two were in the same class at the St. Nicholas School, along with Reema and Nadia. I'd always felt sorry that Layla had lost her second pregnancy and never had another. A child needs a playmate, and I didn't care who heard me say it.

But that dishwasher of Siham's bothered me. It bothered me *so much* inside. I liked Siham dearly—she was sweet and ladylike. Her father was Doctor Al-Medani back home—everyone knew him. He had treated me once as a child, when my brother pushed me down the concrete steps that led to the chicken coop and broke my arm. The Doctor used to travel among the villages that surrounded Jerusalem, and my family summoned him immediately. He came out in the middle of the night, poor man, and smiled at me with his nice eyes while he wrapped and bound my arm and my Aunt Suha and my mother gazed at him in rapture. He was bareheaded and wore trousers and a button-down shirt with a collar, unlike many of the men in the village—like my father—who still wore baggy *sirwal* pants and long, white *hattas* and *i'gals* on their heads.

I told Siham that story when I was first introduced to her, when she moved into the neighborhood, and she almost wept. We hugged right away, and talked for hours about those we had left back home: she missed her parents, and I missed many of my friends and cousins. We talked about how we could arrange visas for them to come to the States, and so we bonded that first day. We became sisters.

But we were still different on many levels. Siham was a lady, the closest thing to the bourgeoisie we had in our South Philadelphia neighborhood. I wasn't one of them, because my family were villagers, though at least—I feel guilty when I think about this, because I know it is wrong—we are not from the refugee camps like poor Layla. But living here in our neat row houses erases most of our differences. Siham and Nader lived in an apartment over the Italian Market, but since Nader split with Layla's husband and bought his own vending cart, they have more money, and were planning to buy a house. I wondered if they would stay in the neighborhood or venture closer to Center City.

Our block sits behind the St. Nicholas of Tolentine Catholic Church and grade school, which all our kids attend, even Huda's kids, though they are Muslims. Our religion doesn't matter here, the way it used to not matter back home before everyone—Jew, Christian, Muslim—thought he had the answer to everything. Here, in America, our water comes in from the same pipe and our sewage exits from the same pipe—here, we are all the same.

At least, until Siham went and convinced Nader that she needed a dishwasher. None of us knew until she invited us to her apartment one afternoon for coffee and cake and a movie. That's how we entertained ourselves in those days, when there was so little to distract us. I stayed at home to raise my four, and that was enough work, thank you. Siham sewed at home for a clothing manufacturer, Huda watched some of the neighbor's children during the day for money, and Layla . . . well, Layla was too nervous and shell-shocked, too sensitive, to be much help to her husband, so she stayed home.

But Saturday afternoons, when our husbands took the boys and went to the Lebanese bookstore and coffee shop on 9th Street—this block of time, these precious few hours belonged to us. We had the girls, of course, but they never attached themselves to us for long. Nadia, Reema, Hanan, and my Aliyah went into a bedroom and shut the door, and soon, we could hear from downstairs the sound of Michael Jackson's or Cyndi Lauper's music. The ceiling above us would shake as they practiced dance steps and choreographed routines. They tore white paper from their notebooks and designed their own line of clothing that was full of bright pink scraps of fabric, zippers, mismatched socks, and big hats. I had pierced Aliyah's ears myself when she was a baby, using a needle heated over the stove and an uncooked potato as its landing spot, but I warned her now that if she ever put a second earring hole in her ears, I would cut them off and leave her deaf. Of course, she just rolled her eyes as usual. Huda tells me that Reema reacts the same way when she tells her not to rip her jeans at the thigh—is it wrong for us to want our girls to look respectable, and not like they live on the streets?

Aliyah cannot believe I used to be a history teacher before I had her and her brothers. I tell her that I left that career for her sake, and the child shrugs like it's not a big deal. My life is no big deal to her. I tell myself that I am pretty smart for learning English so fast when I came here, for finishing college, and for marrying a man who owned a grocery store with four solid walls and a real door, not an aluminum cart on the sidewalk. I tell myself that she will mature soon and see all of this.

We sit in Siham's living room, while the girls are upstairs listening to the crazy Cyndi or to Michael Jackson, who wears one glove for fashion. Back home, during the war, as Huda puts it, we had one glove because we either couldn't afford the other one or had to share a pair with a sibling. We put on a videotape. The Lebanese grocery store rents these out, but Siham and I are the only ones who have VCRs—I bought mine the week after she did, but I paid much less for it. All she had to do, I told her, was to wait for the sales, and not be too hurried to spend. That day, we watched *Aqud al-Lulu* (*The Pearl Necklace*), starring Ghawar and Sabah. Sabah played a village girl whom Ghawar loves, but she doesn't take him seriously. Of course, Sabah's role features many songs, so that her voice can hit its unbelievably high notes.

"Do you know she must be about fifty in this film?" Siham said.

"No!" cried Layla.

"Yes." She nodded knowingly as she bit into her honey cake, then set it down delicately on its pink plate.

"Can it be possible?" I asked. "Look how smooth her skin is."

"Face pulls," Siham said, almost in a whisper.

"NO!" the three of us exclaimed.

"Disgusting," said Huda. "What is so wrong with a few wrinkles? We're not meant to live forever. Is there shame in showing in it?"

"Speak for yourself," I said, touching my fingertips to my cheeks. "In college, the only thing it was fashionable to put on your face was moisturizing cream, because it keeps you young, or whitening cream, so you don't get dark. I still don't wear makeup to this day, except for parties."

"You don't need it, Imm Nabeel," they all reassured me quickly. "Any man would die for those lovely green eyes of yours," Huda added, and the others agreed vehemently and finished off their sweets. After we drained our coffee cups and let the grounds dry inside, Huda read our fortunes for us. She's an expert in this, once predicting when my youngest son would be born. I don't know why I semi-believe in these little superstitious rituals, but maybe it's because I was raised breathing it, accepting it like air in my lungs.

Huda saw a man in Layla's cup—"Not for you, for your daughter, *insh'allah*"—and we all giggled to see how feverishly Layla blushed. She saw windows in my cup—"Symbols of opportunity ahead," she explained—and oval shapes in Siham's. "I'm not too sure about those," she said hesitatingly, holding it out for us to see. The entire inside of the cup was dotted with these ovals, some long and some short, filling the belly of the tiny cup like a rainstorm.

"Maybe you'll get a new polka-dot dress?" I joked.

"*Insh'allah!*" she responded, laughing.

When the movie ended, we moved to help Siham clean up the mess we'd made: the pink coffee cups, the matching cake plates, and the bowls of watermelon seed shells.

"Don't touch a thing," she protested. "I'll put them right into the dishwasher." She tossed out the word casually, but the way she studied us to see if it had had its effect made me sure it was intentional.

Of course we followed her into the kitchen to see this dishwasher. It was large and white and gleaming. We watched her—enviously, I admit—open its wide door, stack her plates inside, and tell us how Nader had decided it was necessary. "He wants us to be *modern*."

Later that evening, I seethed to Abu Nabeel, "Are we not 'modern'?"

"Calm down, *ya* Imm Nabeel. We can have a dishwasher if you like. They are becoming more affordable. Soon, everyone will own one anyway."

"I don't *need* one!" I stormed. "I have two hands to wash my dishes!" And then remembering that he often helped me with this chore and others, I added, "We can do them ourselves, without fancy machines."

He smiled and returned to his *oud*, the one instrument he could sit with for hours, playing and strumming all night. I tried not to encourage it, because he sometimes forgot he had a family living around him when he played, but I did enjoy listening. He was really quite good. The soft tunes filled our home, reaching from Aliyah's room upstairs, where she read day and night, to the basement below, where the boys spent all their time lifting weights and organizing their baseball cards.

As he played, I sat beside him and picked up my new issue of *Money* magazine, which I subscribed to, along with *Good Housekeeping*, *Time* magazine, and the *New York Times* Sunday edition. I did not want to forget all that I had learned in college. My mind drifted from an article on retirement accounts to my friend Samira's dorm room at Temple University. She and I were among five other Arab girls at the university. Her parents were in Lebanon, so she had a dorm room and freedom that I envied. I, on the other hand, only went to Temple because I'd gotten financial aid and the campus was twelve minutes from my parents' house by subway. Even though they pushed me to get a degree, they never would have allowed me to go to a college that required me to leave home. I was lucky to even have the chance, they'd always reminded me.

Nineteen sixty-seven was my senior year, but we spent more time breathing politics than studying for classes and exams. We would gather in Samira's room, because she had a radio, and talk anxiously. What did Syria have planned? What had Gamal Abdel Nasser said in his latest speech? Would the Arabs attack first, or would Israel? Most importantly, would my family return to Palestine when the Arabs won? Was our house still there, as I remembered it, nestled in the stony hills outside of Jerusalem?

When I told Samira I wanted to go back, she lit a cigarette and studied me coolly. "I don't think you would," she finally said. I loved her Lebanese accent, so airy and crisp and glittering with French words, unlike my guttural village dialect, probably the ugliest sound in the world. We always spoke to each other in Arabic, and I tried to memorize her diction and practice later at home as I read from my mother's Bible, the only book in Arabic she'd brought with her.

"Of course I would. It's our home. I haven't seen it in six years."

"You would miss life here, without a doubt. You'd miss your freedom."

"Freedom?" I snorted. "Please. I'm afraid to ask you for a smoke because my parents might smell it on me. Back home, I could run all over the village and not come home till dawn, and my mother at least knew I was safe. Here, she screams at me if I'm not home exactly twenty minutes after she knows my class ends!" I lay back on her floor pillow, and tuned her radio to the news station. "That's why my class schedule, as she knows it, is not exactly accurate."

She just stared at me quietly, blowing smoke elegantly, until I felt prompted to continue. "Why do you think I'm taking summer classes? I'll suffocate in that house until September comes back around."

We listened to the news broadcast for a while. The hostilities intensified. Street battles took place every day in Jerusalem, and Nasser's speeches became more and more belligerent as he called for Arab unity and war on Israel. "When the Arabs win, we'll go back to Jerusalem without a doubt," I said firmly. "My parents agree on that—we're only here temporarily, although Baba wants me to rush to finish my degree so I can get a job as soon as we go back."

Samira tapped her ash on a small dish. "I hope I never go back. Lebanon is changing for the worse, according to my mother. It's becoming . . . well, never mind."

On the subway ride home, I thought about her last words furiously. Lebanon was changing, she meant, because the Palestinians who had fled or been expelled in 1948 had landed there. We would have joined them in 1963, if my mother's brother hadn't sent us money on a regular basis from Guatemala, where he'd fled in 1948, or if the French priest in a nearby Christian village had not helped us and several other families get to France and then to America. But those who hadn't known people like Uncle Hannah and Père Phillipe had gone to the Western bank of the river or up to Lebanon, or even south toward the Sinai. And they had no money, had salvaged so little from their lives. So of course, people like Samira's family probably had had their comfortable lives disrupted by our tragedy down south.

Even now, as I sat staring blankly at the pages of *Money* magazine, I was startled by the wave of resentment that washed over me, drowning out the soft waves of Abu Nabeel's music, making my heart beat a pace faster. My head started to hurt, and I saw the oval pattern of Siham's coffee cup swirling before my eyes. I think that this feeling will always be with me, like my accent. Though gentler and softer than either Huda's or Layla's, it would never quite disappear, no matter how hard I focused. It would surface only occasionally, when I encountered difficult words like "Robitussin" or "chameleon" or "salmon," or when I became agitated, watching friends in our circle try to rise above us.

"Abu Nabeel!" I said, standing up and putting on my shoes. "Abu Nabeel!"

He paused, his hand suspended over the strings, and looked at me expectantly.

"I'm going back to see Siham for a few minutes. Your boys are in the basement and your daughter is reading in her room."

He nodded as if in a daze and returned immediately to his playing.

I strode to Siham's, covering the four blocks in only a few minutes. I wasn't sure what I would say to her. Perhaps I would tell her she had forgotten where we all came from, had forgotten that we had landed with one bag each and an endless supply of miserable memories. And that our common bond was our only salve. I didn't know, but I would do something.

She saw me from the basement window of the flower shop, tapped on the screen, and yelled up, "The door is open. Come in. I'm just taking down the clothes." The owner had allowed them access to the basement to do laundry.

I walked in and sat down at her kitchen table. Besides the sink, next to the glorious dishwasher, was a little bowl filled with several rings and two gold bracelets. They were made of Arabic gold, with its 21 karat bright yellow color. I imagined suddenly what Samira's mother back in Lebanon must have looked like—her hands bejeweled with large rings, her neck encircled with chains of gold, her hair dyed a deep red henna and her heavily mascaraed eyes watching the news about a skirmish in the refugee camps. She would turn to her husband and exclaim, "*C'est impossible* how these Palestinians are ruining us!"

My father could have been wealthy also—he had owned half the farmland in the village! God knows what it was worth now, especially in a prime location like Jerusalem's outskirts. But now, in Philadelphia, we shared even our walls with our neighbors. I counted pennies painstakingly, because I had four children who eventually would need college money, and I rarely bought new dresses or fancy clothes—and here was Siham with a fancy, expensive new machine, to remind me of what had been lost!

I walked over to the dishwasher and opened its door. The pink dishes from this afternoon were still stacked inside, but they hadn't been washed. Perhaps she was waiting to put her dinner dishes in there as well. I pulled out my cup, and saw again the little windows that Huda had pointed out to me. I hoped it was true. Then I pulled out Siham's cup, and stared at the dizzying ovals again. They suddenly looked like little teardrops to me. I glanced above her stove, where a blue stone hung above the range. Siham had blue stones hanging all over her house—above the door, above the stove, in every window and every bedroom. But, as I heard her coming up the basement steps, lugging a basket, I closed the dishwasher door and then . . . and then I said a curse anyway, against her fancy dishwasher and her modernity. The words formed in the blackest corner of my heart and were purged from my lips, hanging like dark clouds in Siham's kitchen.

"I hope I didn't startle you, Imm Nabeel," she said, setting her basket down on the chair and moving over to the coffee pot. "I was hoping it was Nader. He's late coming home from work. I guess he went to the coffee shop."

"I don't think so. Abu Nabeel has been home for over two hours. If they had all planned a game, surely he wouldn't miss it." She looked confused, so I quickly added, "God bring him home safely. I'm not staying long, so don't make any coffee for me."

"Why not?" she protested politely, filling the pot halfway with water. "I'm finished with most of my work. I even have dinner ready, so you can eat with us when Nader gets home."

"No, no. I don't want to trouble you."

"Why did you come? Is everything OK?" she asked then, peering at me curiously as she dumped the water out and started folding her laundry, piling the clothes on the chair beside her.

Blushing, I struggled to think of an answer. "Because I wanted to tell you what a fancy queen you may think you are," I wanted to say, but now I did not feel nearly as powerful as I had while walking over here. Instead, I felt satiated, strangely triumphant. And a bit silly. What was wrong with me? Had I actually planned to put her in her place by coming over here? What had I been thinking?

Her kitchen clock chimed softly then. "Eight o'clock?" Her voice rose worriedly. "Where *is* he?"

"I'm sure he's fine." I headed for the front door. "Maybe he stopped somewhere else."

"Are you sure you don't want to sit with me?" she asked, and it was the desperate tone in her voice that made me turn to look at her. Her lips were pressed tightly together and her dark eyes flitted between the clock and the door nervously. I would have stayed—I honestly would have—but just then her hand reached up and clutched the heavy gold chain around her neck. She looped her index finger around it and distractedly slid her finger up and down the chain.

"I really have to go."

I rebuked myself all the way home, thinking shamefully of the curse I had uttered. Why did I resent her? Because she liked to show off? And I . . . I was no better than Samira and her mother, the way I still thought of Layla and even Reema, both of whom had grown up in the camps. Somewhere between leaving Palestine and having children, I had developed a class conscience. College education had apparently had no effect on me! Here I was, putting the Evil Eye on people who bought fancy machines, when I had never even believed in such nonsense.

I shook my head vigorously as I walked, shaking away the silliness I had succumbed to. As I fumbled with the key to my front door, I mumbled, "God forgive me. And help me." It was logic, really, a corrective measure: I had invoked God's name for negative reasons, and now I did so for positive ones.

Abu Nabeel was on the phone when I walked in, his *oud* lying on the carpet, face down, its bloated belly swelled in the air.

"Yes, yes, she just walked in. We'll drive down and get you now, Siham."

"Siham?" I tossed my purse on the table. "*B'khair, insh'allah?* I just came from their apartment."

"The police called right after you left. Nader had a car accident on the way home from the coffee shop. She needs to get to St. Agnes on Broadway."

I stood there dumbly as he put on his shoes and his cardigan and yelled for Aliyah to come downstairs. "We'll take her to Huda's; she can stay with Reema. I don't want her at the hospital in case . . . you know what I'm saying."

Still I did not move; I only stood, staring down at the *oud* on the floor. It had only been a five-minute walk back home. Why hadn't I stayed with Siham? I imagined her getting that phone call, probably as I was walking home and regretting what I had done.

Aliyah raced down the steps, urged by the high pitch of her father's voice. She slipped on her shoes without a word when he told her what happened, though I saw her face become pale. They both glanced at the front door, and then back at me impatiently. "*Y'allah, ya Imm Nabeel!* We don't have a second to waste!" my husband called.

I pushed myself forward, walking toward them like a criminal going to the gallows, thoroughly ashamed and deeply afraid.

An Afternoon in Jerusalem

I wondered if I should do the melodramatic thing and burn Kareem's picture. That's what would happen in an Arabic soap opera, with an actress, her eyes lined Cleopatra-style (à la Liz Taylor) with kohl, sniffling as she set a match to the photo of her heartless lover, the flame reflecting dramatically against her hennaed hair. An American soap actress would do the same, tossing it into the fireplace and watching the flames lick and blacken his fair skin and blond hair. But my apartment didn't have a fireplace, and besides, I needed to do something unscripted, hard, real, something that maybe hurt, like bursting a blister before the white liquid inside made it explode. It was still pain, but at least you held the pin.

My mother's words still echoed in my mind, weaving their way from the telephone wires and carving themselves into the walls of my memory. It had been eight in the morning when Mama called, while I was slipping into my shoes, smudging on eyeshadow, and sipping my coffee. My routine abruptly stopped (though the Santa Claus mug did *not* dramatically crash to the floor) when she told me about Kareem.

I threw off my shoes, calmly rested the mug on my dresser, and sat on my bed as I listened. I've always been calm in a crisis, like the time my brother Nabeel broke his nose. Someone on Mifflin Street had called him a "dirty Arab" and smashed his face with a Wiffle ball bat. I had been reading *Anne of Green Gables* on my front step when Nicki Donato and a bunch of the other kids ran up and gasped out that Nabeel was bleeding. My friends usually tease me for being quiet, but something ruptured within me. I sprinted the six blocks to Mifflin Street, beat up the kid as well as his two cousins with the bat, marched Nabeel home, and called my mother at Auntie Siham's house. Of course, the kid and his brother called me "crazy terrorist" for a while, but they stayed away from my family after that.

After I hung up with Mama, I made two other phone calls: my editor, to cancel my morning meeting, and Nadia, to tell her that I would not be coming over for dinner that evening.

"Why not, Aliyah?" she whined, and I hated lying about feeling ill, especially when she'd been confined to her bed for months since her car accident. She'd become grumpy, and I felt guilty for forgetting to spend time with her. I hung up quickly and, unsure of what else to do, I pulled out my box of photos from that summer.

"He's marrying Fattin, the daughter of your father's neighbor from Ramallah," Mama had said, her words bringing back the image of Fattin's chubby cheeks and hooded eyes to my mind. I imagined her face and then Kareem's, with his dark eyes and thick black lashes about which medieval poets on horseback would have composed ghazals had they adorned the face of a woman.

Kareem's eyes gazed back at me now from the gloss of one photograph in particular. I was in that photo too, wearing the red, embroidered scarf that he bought for me that afternoon in the Old City. We stood in front of Damascus Gate, staring at the camera, though perhaps I should have been looking intently at the person holding it. Kareem's eyes in the photo are dark pools of molasses. Mine are closed.

I still had the scarf, folded neatly on the top shelf of my closet, where I kept a lot of things I didn't want to look at, but didn't want to throw away. Some things I kept closer to me; the golden crucifix pendant he'd given me when we first started "talking"—as the Palestinians called it, because it was never "dating"—still hung around my neck. I could never throw that away. I had been taught how to respect religious objects: to kiss the statue of Mary if it ever fell off the shelf to the ground, to press the crucifix or the image of Jesus to my lips when I needed help.

He had given me the scarf with a flourish that day in front of Damascus Gate. "To my American sweetheart," he'd said, and draped it around my shoulders.

I'd flinched, and reminded him that I was an *Arab*-American. There was a hyphen there, connecting the two things that created me: the one that drew me to him and the other that kept me at a distance.

"Yes . . ." And he smiled to pose for the picture. The camera was raised, and even though I knew the flash was coming, I'd blinked.

I pulled myself off the bed, still wearing my pantsuit. Shoeless, I went back to the closet and pulled down my journals this time. I had spent an entire year writing endlessly about Kareem, filling pages madly, obsessively, even in the middle of the night, hands trembling, fingers itching, reaching for the notebook and the desk lamp. The words inked onto the ruled pages, stacked tightly like bricks, had formed a defensive barricade against invading thoughts of him. I had not written about him for months, but now I wanted to read.

The first page was actually about my grandfather, Baba's father, with whom I had lived in Ramallah that summer. Sidi had never left the West Bank, not once in his entire life—and was happy that way. "If you want to see me," he told us, his grandchildren in the States during obligatory Christmas and Easter phone calls, "you come here." My grandmother had died years ago, and Sidi never remarried, learning instead to cook for himself and to wash his own clothes, making wives in Ramallah look resentfully at their own husbands.

The date of that summer's first entry was June 3rd: *It is hot and sticky in Ramallah, my ankles are swollen like those of a pregnant woman, and the city just announced that the water would be cut off for the rest of the evening and perhaps even tomorrow morning. Sidi laughed at my face as he translated some of the words in English for me (like I'm supposed to know how to say "water reservoir" in Arabic). "Now you can't have that long, hot shower like you Americans like to take!"*

That was one of the problems, I thought, flipping pages. Mama and Baba always spoke to me about "back home," and that was why I had finally gone that summer. Mama's parents had brought her to the States during one of the wars, but died before they could return. Sidi, Baba's father, had never left. His land and farm outside Jerusalem had been seized to build settlements, so he moved his family to Ramallah. So I wasn't going to the home Baba had been born in. I never could return to that because it had been replaced by a walled-in city to which my dark skin and last name denied me access. Even worse, I couldn't gain access to Sidi's and Kareem's world, partly because of my Americanness, my accent, and partly because they didn't really see me as part of their lives. "I feel like you just floated into my life," Kareem said once, "and you haven't settled down yet."

My fingers found July 29th, the day inked in a dark blue pen that had eventually faded and been replaced with a red marker, the first instrument my fingers found in the bottom of my bag that moment. That was the day I had not returned to since I'd written it, but now I scoured the pages:

It is a cool day. The intense sunshine bleached the already-white stone balcony of Sidi's house, but a light breeze made it bearable. A strong glare bounced off the Mercedes taxis driving by and seared my eyes. Kareem arrived, wearing sunglasses and the pair of Levi's blue jeans that I had brought for him from the States. I'm glad he's wearing them. He asked if I wanted to go to Jerusalem for the afternoon, to the Old City.

"I want to show it to you. I want you to see it through my eyes." It was a nice gesture, but I didn't want to tell him that I had grown tired of waiting for him to take me, and that I'd hired a private taxi to drop me

off the week before. So I lied, smiled, and then listened intently when he said someone was coming with us. Fattin, a friend of his from college. "We'll pick her up on the way in the taxi."

"Why does she have to come?" I don't like Fattin. I've met her and her mother before and they don't seem like the kind of women I could befriend easily or talk to comfortably. I think Fattin feels the same about me.

He leaned against the balcony rail, twisting his fingers around the ironwork. "Because it's not proper, Aliyah. You know that."

Funny what he thinks is proper. When I visited Ramallah last year with my father and first met Kareem, he had no problem taking me out to cafés and to dinner all over the city. Now that we are "talking," he suddenly frets about social conventions that probably exist only in his mind. I think I hate the word "proper" more than any other.

I was silent during the taxi ride, not listening to Kareem and Fattin as they talked to each other across my body, which sat between them like an ineffective barrier. I'd always been gifted with the talent to block out everything around me (my mother insists that is why a car once ran over my foot when I was a child, because I heard neither its honks from several feet away nor her shrieks from our stoop). And so I let them chat happily while I slipped into my own world, remembering my own trip to Jerusalem last week.

My fingers flipped back, back, until I landed upon July 23rd.

Today, I strolled around Jerusalem alone, breathing in its history and observing its modernity, like people selling traditional sesame bread along with bottles of Diet Coke. I bought some flat loaves of sesame, and the boy who sold them at his cart resembled Kareem—the same, big dark eyes and intense squint, and the wrinkle between his brows. He caught me staring and winked brazenly. I laughed and continued on my way, feeling like a young Benjamin Franklin, newly landed, walking through Philadelphia with his loaves of bread and pondering his virtues.

I dodged hordes of tourists and eager, teenaged salespeople who wore Hilfiger sneakers and pushed carts filled with scarves, crates of live chickens, and piles of vegetables. Finally, I arrived at the Haram al-Sharif: I know that the men worshipped in Al-Aqsa Mosque and women in the Dome of the Rock, but I still hesitated to enter the Dome. An older woman wearing a blue dress and a hijab passed by and, noticing the crucifix around my neck, took my arm. "Come in, come in." I smiled at her and shook my head, but she took a scarf out of her dress pocket and handed it to me. "Our God is the same. Welcome and see." She showed me how to wrap it around my hair, tucking in every strand. It was not nearly as long and flowing as hers, but it would suffice. We took our shoes off at the door and I insisted on observing from the back. She nodded. "I will go now. I have a lot to pray for. My son was martyred last year and my daughter just lost her job." Before I could summon up enough Arabic to offer her my sympathies, she was gone, weaving her way among the throng of women.

I stayed behind, sitting quietly and breathing in the scent of musk. The room was enormous, and beautiful arabesques adorned the walls and interior Dome, whose golden exterior I had always seen crowning pictures of Jerusalem. Now I was here, finally inside the picture.

My finger rubbed the golden cross around my neck, and I couldn't wait to tell Kareem about being here, about the uniform movements of the women prostrating themselves and touching their heads to the ground. Voices rose, synchronous, unified.

I closed my journal and lay on my bed, remembering that day in the mosque, the orderliness of the service and the unison of female prayer. There was a power there that I identified with—it had been the first time I felt comfortable in Palestine. But why had I felt like sharing that moment with Kareem? I don't think I ever really did—what had stopped me? Maybe it should remain what it was already, closed off to some, only open to others who really wanted to enter.

It annoyed me that I had chosen to jump so quickly to immerse myself in Palestine, in him, in his environment. Had he ever really shown an enthusiasm for knowing where I came from, what motivated me? How would he have liked Philadelphia? I imagined him strolling down South Street with me, gasping at every Kool-Aid-blue-haired waif in a babydoll dress, biker shorts, and Doc Martens, walking with her tattooed and pierced boyfriend/girlfriend/partner. He would stand, shocked, before the window of CondomNation, peering in at the boxes of penis-shaped pasta, blushing furiously when he realized what it was. Sitting with my friends from the university, sipping black coffee and arguing about Derrida and Said, about Virginia Woolf's suicide and Amiri Baraka's politics, and about what "orientalism" really meant. He would have fallen asleep or become irritable and insisted on going home, and my friends would have shaken their heads sadly as we walked away, wondering, "How did Aliyah wind up with such an old-fashioned guy?"

The photograph stared up at me, my eyes closed and his dark ones open, his lips smiling for the faceless person behind the camera.

I called Nadia, ashamed of my earlier lie. "Kareem is getting married, to Fattin. I just found out a couple of hours ago. Can I still come over later for dinner?"

"You sound terrible. Why don't you just come now?"

"You sure?" The car accident had happened in the winter, and her shattered legs had not quite healed.

"Just come, for Christ's sake. We could both use the company."

I stopped at D'Alessandro's corner market and bought a bottle of nonalcoholic wine, for a laugh, but also because she was still on some painkillers.

Auntie Siham let me in, and I could tell right away that she knew about Kareem. "Didn't take Nadia long to tell you, huh? I mean, come *on*, girl!" I yelled in the direction of her bedroom. "I only live ten minutes away. Does all of Palestine know, too?"

"Yeah. And they all said, '*Y'allah, get over it*,'" came the response.

I giggled along with Auntie Siham, not because I thought it was funny, but because I didn't want to make Nadia feel bad for a below-the-belt crack. I helped Auntie open the wine bottle, then carried it and two glasses on a tray into Nadia's small room. She was watching *Days of Our Lives*.

She smiled up at me from her nest in the maroon comforter. Her brown hair, streaked with golden highlights, was tied up in a sloppy bun on top of her head, and her dark eyeliner was smudged. She shifted to the side, grimacing, to make room for me on the foot of the bed. "Remember when me, you, Hanan, and Reema used to watch this every day and our moms would come in and turn it off?"

"And tell us that these American shows were filth and would ruin us."

"Didn't they? Weren't we all waiting for a Bo Brady who liked to eat *malfouf* and smoke *narghile* and sweep us off our feet?" Her face looked more serious than her playful voice, and I had no response for her. She pointed to my neck and asked, "Why are you still wearing that?"

I tucked the crucifix back in my blouse.

"I wish it had worked out for you," she said after a while, running her finger up and down the chilled glass, interrupting the beads of sweat as they made little tracks down its side.

"I tried really hard . . ."

"I know, Aliyah. But does it really matter? We're different, and that's it. They tell us we're not Americans and, sure, we listen to the music and drink the coffee." She yawned. "We're just different, and that's OK."

"But I want to be *more* than that," I insisted. "That summer, I fit in. I really liked it there, Nadia, for the first time."

She just looked at me sadly and pushed her glass away, wincing as her leg bumped the small table beside the bed. Her face transformed from looking pained to looking furious. "Damnit!"

"You OK?"

"I never should have gotten into that car with George," she snapped.

She didn't mean it, I knew. George was deeply in love with her, and the shelf above her bed was stuffed with little plush toys and cards from him. One teddy bear dressed as a nurse was cradled in the arms of a koala bear, who held a heart-shaped, plastic balloon in one hand: "Get Well Soon."

"He's a great guy, Nadia."

She didn't reply, just stared stonily at the television.

"What's wrong?"

"My ass is falling asleep from sitting in this bed all day. I'll go back to work in a month, but still—I need physical therapy and . . . there's just so much that's gone wrong."

"Don't shut him out, Nadia. It wasn't his fault."

"Yes, it was!" she blurted, her face flushing a bright red. "He wasn't watching the road—he turned to talk to Hanan and John. What would my mother have done, without me? My father's already gone—what would she have done?"

I remembered that night, the sound of my mother's voice when she woke me up to tell me about the accident. The first thing she'd sobbed out was, "Thank God it wasn't you in the car, Aliyah!" I resented that comment, because as much as I knew what propelled her to say it, its intensity embarrassed me. An SUV had run a stop sign and plowed into George's car, or perhaps it was George who'd run the stop sign. Nobody knew for sure, but only Nadia had been seriously hurt. Her recovery seemed miraculous, and we were all so happy for Auntie Siham. Hanan, Reema, and I had spent days taking turns sleeping at the hospital.

I suddenly wished I hadn't come, that I could be back in my apartment, where I could cry privately. But I stayed, and we finished *Days* and even *Passions*, and both our glasses remained untouched.

When Nadia fell asleep, I chatted with her mother at her kitchen table, whispering like confidantes. "She's very depressed, Aliyah, but it will be OK."

"But she shouldn't push George away."

"It's for the best."

"He really loves her. He calls me sometimes to ask about her—"

"It's for the best, Aliyah," she repeated with finality.

Back at my apartment, I pulled out the journals again and sat at my kitchen table, the ceiling fan whirring above my head. I searched again for the day about Jerusalem, not the time I spent alone, but rather the time with Kareem and Fattin. They had taken me first to the Church of the Holy Sepulchre; I found the corresponding photograph of Kareem and myself standing before the tomb that dominates the entrance, and the brass lamps that dangle above it and emanate thick incense. My hand was on his sleeve, my smile wide, and for the first time, upon looking closely, I can see that his own hands are clenched. The look on his face is not a free, genuine happiness, but uneasiness—his eyes are looking off to the left.

July 29th: At the Holy Sepulchre, Kareem explained the various sections of the church to me, like the crack in the wall where a shard of wood jutted out. A sheet of glass protected the entire crevice. "They say it's a piece of the cross," he said, " and they saved it here in the church."

"Do you believe that?" I asked skeptically.

"Of course," Fattin snapped, then recovered and laughed. "I mean, it's the story we are always taught—at least, that Kareem and I were taught."

"Yes, we don't really question these things, Aliyah," Kareem said gently. I wanted to kill him.

"Well, I didn't grow up next door to a two-thousand-year-old church," I quipped. "The Catholic Church near my house has only been there since 1940s." But of course, I understood Fattin's message—she doesn't think I am a good fit for her dear, dear friend. I was withdrawn for the rest of the afternoon, and Kareem looked at me with concern and put his hand on my arm during the cab ride, in full view of Fattin who would be sure to return home directly and tell her mother.

I took the crucifix off now, pressed it to my lips, and laid it on the table. It was scratched badly, but I would polish it carefully and give it to Nadia, who needed it more than I did.

I had worn it six months too long, six months since Kareem had called me to say it wouldn't work, that we should stop "talking."

I'd never told him about that day in Jerusalem—my private adventure, just me and the city's walls, cemeteries, churches, and mosques, the afternoon before the one when I first knew that we were too different after all. Before I really understood that my stumbling Arabic didn't cut it, and that I would carelessly blink and lose him to an eye that framed us both but remained, itself, invisible.

HANAN

Preparing a Face

There will be time, there will be time
To prepare a face to meet the faces that you meet.
— T. S. Eliot

Her cousin was coming to America, and Hanan was again reminded by her mother that, though she'd never met Rola, "Blood runs deep." Mama always said this maxim as if she'd invented it, similar to her other famous decree, "Oil and water don't mix," to refer to Americans and Arabs. She said these things in her clipped accent that Hanan's friends insisted was "enchanting." But for Hanan, it was yet another difference between them. A symbol that she didn't speak Arabic all that well and that her mother's English was still burdened after twenty-six years in America. But Mama just dismissed it and said Hanan was always being so dramatic and why didn't she just stop it?

The accusation of drama usually ended such conversations, the kind that started when Mama said something that made Hanan feel inadequate. "Hanan, when you serve coffee to guests, you start first with oldest person. Why you always forget? You almost have college degree, but you cannot remember so simple a thing? You insulted Abu Hatem." And it wasn't even her words so much as that clucking, hushed sound that she forced through firmly pressed lips, her tongue rattling against the cage of her mouth.

Whenever her mother rebuked her for committing these cultural transgressions, Hanan wanted to pound her head against the wall. She knew the words and the embarrassment over what she'd done would pop into her mind at the most unexpected moments. It was at such moments, sitting in the subway car or reading her email at work, that the memory of her mother's lopsided frown and flared nostrils would hit her like a punch in the stomach.

The worst was the recurring memory of the time she had taken a seat next to her elderly uncle Ibrahim during a family gathering and had crossed her ankle over her knee. While she tried to chat with her impenetrable uncle, everyone else in the room—her parents, cousins, aunts, and uncles—had either glared at her or shifted uncomfortably in their seats. Only later that evening, when everyone had gone home and she was washing dishes for her mother, had she been told that the bottom of her foot had been plainly visible and facing Uncle Ibrahim.

"So?" she'd said, using her fingers to funnel a stream of warm water into the belly and down the insides of a serving bowl.

"You *never* do that!" her mother had exclaimed. "It's an insult to show someone the bottom of your foot—everyone in that room is going to be talking about it. My brother Ibrahim will probably never come here again."

"Mama," Hanan persisted, her irritation flooding over her like the water now spilling over the sides of the bowl. "Mama, how can he be mad at me for something I didn't even know I was doing?"

"Crazy girl," her mother muttered, and stalked over to the sink and slammed the faucet handle shut. Then she walked out of the kitchen and upstairs. Hanan could hear the stairs creaking and a bed-room door slam. Defeated, she tossed the sponge into the sink and headed upstairs herself. As she passed her parent's door, she heard her mother's high-pitched, fierce tones. Her dad's voice was muffled and soft, as usual. She knew that he'd come to her tomorrow and give her a kiss on the cheek, then pat the same spot he'd kissed as if to make sure it stuck, and tell her not to worry about it.

Hanan closed her own bedroom door, and then, still hearing Mama's rants, she stacked the small decorative pillows on her bed along the bottom edge of her door to keep it out.

When she was finally in complete silence, sitting on her bed and gazing at the pillows lined up like soldiers at the front line of a cul-tural war, when she finally felt safe in her fortified room, she decided she was not an Arab. Her father was an American, born to Arab par-ents, but her mother hadn't been born here—she'd grown up in the hilly town of Ramallah, had fled a series of wars, had left behind camps strewn with shrapnel, legless corpses, wailing women, and eyes too weary to weep. But Hanan had been born right here, in Philadel-phia, in St. Agnes Hospital on Broad Street, and she had lived here all her life, next to Mrs. Carpetti and her four cats who kept eating the flowers on her windowsill, right down the street from the corner deli, owned by Mr. Spinelli with the white hair who's always asked her when she was a kid, "You dark-haired cutie-pie, you sure you not Italian?" before giving her a chocolate candy. This was where *she* was from, and who cared if she shoved her foot in someone's face?

The morning that they drove to the airport to pick up her cousin Rola, Hanan and her mother hardly spoke. Hanan drove the two of them in her small red Ford Escort, which she'd bought after dropping out of college and getting a job in a clothing store. Her mother had her own car, a Lincoln Continental so large that she could barely see over the steering wheel, and she did drive, but only within a five-mile radius of their home so the neighbors at least would see her. She was afraid to venture much farther than that. Hanan had almost laughed when Mama had said, "The airport is too far. You drive to bring Rola?" She'd wanted to say "no," but she was curious about her cousin, who had never been to America, according to Mama. She wondered how much she would have in common with Rola, or if she'd have anything in common at all. Would her cousin expect her to be a docile Arab girl, the lone flower on the dark terrain of wild America? She wondered just how wholly Rola bought the package of irreverent Americans, which she was sure Aunt Warda, who was probably a carbon copy of Mama, had taught her.

"Blood runs deep." She recalled her mother's words as she drove in the left lane on I-95, passing over the landscape of the row houses along the gleaming Delaware River, then into the industrial area in the southwestern part of the city, *her* city, her home and roots.

"Hanan, go out of this lane," her mother commanded. "Too fast. We want to be there alive."

For some reason, that calm, haughty exterior jangled her nerves, even though Hanan was used to it. She swerved sharply, spitefully, into the middle lane, hoping to unnerve her mother.

"Crazy girl," her mother said calmly, clicking her tongue against her teeth reproachfully.

"I'll show you crazy, Mama," Hanan laughed, swerving back into the left lane, then back again to the middle.

"Why are you so crazy?" her mother asked her in Arabic.

"Because I'm *your* daughter!" Hanan replied, in English, on purpose.

Then the sirens deafened her, and she didn't even have to look in the mirror to see the glare from the cop's flashing lights. She slammed the steering wheel over and over while she pulled the car onto the shoulder.

"Goddamnit!" she shrieked as she shuffled through her purse for her license and registration. In her mirror she could see the cop pull over behind her, descend from his car, and approach her with a slow, superior gait.

"Don't blame this on God," her mother started to say, but Hanan cut her off.

"Just shut up! OK? Shut up and don't say a word." She lowered her window and waited for the cop, then glanced quickly at her mother, whose grief-stricken expression slowly turned stony and cold. "I'm going to pay for that," she thought to herself. "Oh, god-damnit."

They arrived forty minutes late to the airport and found Rola by the baggage claims, watching the conveyor belt attentively. This had to be her cousin, Hanan thought, taking in her pale, thin face, long, glossy black hair, her long, straight nose, similar to the one Hanan had inherited from her own mother, and the thick black eyebrows that had been tamed and shaped into smooth arches. Hanan uncon-sciously slid a finger over her own unruly brows, her cosmetic neme-sis, which grew faster than she could pluck them.

Her mother had already approached Rola and was kissing her cheeks warmly. "How is my sister? How is your father? And your brothers?" she was asking, firing off the questions rapidly. "How is the rest of the family in Ramallah? Do they visit your grandfather's grave once a month—I told them to never forget to do that! God rest his soul . . . if I was there, his spirit would never feel abandoned."

Hanan wanted to roll her eyes, but Rola had wrapped her arm around her aunt and was listening attentively. They barely noticed Hanan, so intensely was her mother chattering, and when Rola fi-nally glanced at her, she looked her over summarily and then re-turned her attention to Hanan's mother.

Hanan stood there a few seconds longer, then became suddenly pissed off. She walked away over to a soda machine and got a Diet Coke. When she'd retrieved it and popped the can open, her mother and cousin were heading in her direction, her cousin pulling a large suitcase on wheels and a smaller bag over her shoulder.

"Hanan, where you go? Why you walk away?" her mother asked in an irritated tone. "I turn, you disappear."

Hanan wished she could.

"This is your cousin, Rola."

That was how Rola entered their lives, gracefully, beautifully, everyone's delight, the princess presiding over her court at the dinner Mama held for her that same night. The family—everyone from the frail Uncle Ibrahim to her cousin Lana, her German husband, and their three black-haired, hazel-eyed children—flocked to their house and were served up a huge dinner and equal portions of Rola's words.

"I finished my bachelor's degree in Amman," she chatted easily, "and I used to go home to Ramallah for the summers. But now I want a master's and I want to do the program here in the States." Her Arabic was beautiful, unstilted, and dropped from her lips softly and demurely, in that Audrey Hepburn-goes-Arabic tone. Hanan told herself not to be silly, because Rola had grown up speaking Arabic and hadn't tried, futilely, to learn it at Sunday afternoon language classes at the local mosque in North Philadelphia, where they taught you to recite the Qur'an even though you were Christian. She didn't mind because the teacher was nice to her and gave her supplemental readings, and the other kids in the class treated her like everyone else. They all had parents who, like her mother, were forcing Arabic down their throats. But the words were too hard and the grammar too complicated and, one week, after a snowstorm stopped her from going to class, she never returned. The teacher called her parents to see what was wrong, and they feebly lied, claiming that she was so busy with other activities. Her mother had been furious because Mr. Ahmad was "such a nice, nice man" and Hanan was "so, so selfish," but she remained stubborn and the subject eventually faded. Sure, she could sometimes understand a lot of it, when people spoke slowly, but it wasn't the same as wearing it like a second skin.

When dinner was over and the family had relocated to the living room, Hanan stayed in the kitchen with Mama to help prepare the tea. She infused the boiling tea with peppermint leaves, wiped down her mother's best silver-plated tray, then arranged the short tea glasses on it. Her mother was busy putting the leftover food into Tupperware containers and didn't pay her any attention. Through the door to the living room, Hanan heard Uncle Ibrahim telling a joke in Arabic and then a burst of laughter from the family. She thought to herself that she'd never felt so alone in the midst of so many people.

The aroma of the tea surged up at her and she poured it into the cups, one by one. "I'll take this in, Mama."

Just then, Rola strolled into the kitchen, her face a rosy red and her black eyes bright. "Need any help, Auntie? Hanan?"

"No," Hanan responded. "I'm just going to take this tea in."

"Rola," her mother interjected quickly, "why don't you serve the tea? Last time Hanan did it, she served the little kids before the guests!"

"I went around the room from right to left," Hanan exclaimed in her own defense, but the knowing smile that her mother and Rola shared was enough. "Fine, go ahead. I actually have to be somewhere anyway." She walked out of the kitchen, out of the house, though before the door closed, she heard her mother say, "That's how she is, my American daughter—if she doesn't like something, she leaves. Too busy for us stupid Arabs. She thinks she hurts us by doing that."

"It's not you I'm thinking about!" she wanted to scream, but closed her lips and walked the six blocks to the used bookstore on South Street where she usually went to hang out. She flipped open her cell phone and called her friend John, who agreed to meet her in a few minutes. Hanan realized that the tone of her voice had probably freaked him out, because John never went anywhere at the last minute. She grabbed a paperback off the shelf and settled into a chair to read.

Peter, the burly, red-haired owner, nodded at her from behind the counter. "Just want to tell you the boys are on the prowl." He owned three cats that often roamed the bookstore, including a fat Persian that had made the store semi-famous in this part of the city. Once Hanan had pulled a heavy book off the shelf and found the cat curled up in the small, cozy space between the volumes, protected by a fortress of pages and words.

"No problem. I actually don't mind the company," she replied and opened the book she'd snatched. It was a collection of T. S. Eliot's poems, and she automatically flipped through until she found "The Love Song of J. Alfred Prufrock"—her favorite poem, especially when she was in a self-pitying mood.

At that moment, Peter's fat Persian snuggled up next to her. She stroked his back, wondering what was taking John so long. He ambled in twenty minutes later, looking pensive and haggard as usual. He saw her on the couch and, running his hand through his thick hair, immediately asked, "Coffee?"

The South Street Café was just a block away, and they settled at a corner table with their white mugs of hot coffee. Hanan listened to his woes about the slow process of writing his doctoral dissertation in sociology at the University of Pennsylvania. When he'd finished telling her about uncaring thesis advisors and classmates who sabotaged each other's research, Hanan announced, "I think my mom gave birth to the wrong daughter."

He offered appropriately timed grunts as she shared her story, then asked, "But she'll be gone soon, right?"

"Yeah, but I don't know when. I don't know why she came now, when she has no clue if she'll be accepted into a program yet. She's waiting for decisions from Stanford, Penn, and some other Ivy League big-wigs."

"Don't diss the Ivy's," he said sarcastically, flashing his University of Pennsylvania ring in her face.

"You haven't even gotten your PhD yet!" she exclaimed. "How did you get a ring?"

He shrugged and asked, "So what are we going to do about your goody two-sandals cousin from the deserts of Arabia?" He leaned forward conspiratorially.

"Don't diss the Arabs."

"Touché." He bowed his head low to the table. "Let me try to re-deem myself: How about we show your cousin an evening on the town, you know, paint the town red and all that?"

Hanan pondered this thought. Her mother always hated it when she went out to clubs and parties, or just out with her friends. "We are Arabs," she'd always say, "not Americans! This is not what we do!"

"What's wrong with going dancing?" Hanan would argue back, wanting to truly understand this mysterious dividing line between Arabs and Americans, who faced off against each other in her mother's mind like boxing opponents. In Mama's mind, they stood in opposite corners, glaring at each other, waiting for the fight to start— in Hanan's life, however, they were constantly dueling it out.

Her mother never gave her an adequate answer. The "I never had the luxury to go dancing" and "We were too busy fleeing from the sol-diers to go dancing" logic never seemed reasonable, especially when Hanan flipped on the Arabic satellite TV stations to shows and music videos in which people—dressed like runway models—danced to Arabic, American, and even French and Indian music. And so Hanan spent at least one Saturday night a month with John and her other friends, hopping from club to club—from a disco joint, to a hip-hop club, to a blues bar—and she never got home before 2 A.M. And al-ways, like a ghost haunting a house, a little, brown face would appear in the front window as Hanan's car pulled into the driveway. It would quickly disappear behind the curtains and, as she opened the front door that had been left unlocked for her, Hanan would hear her mother's bedroom door slam upstairs.

She and John stayed out late that very evening, talking and meet-ing up with some of their other friends, anything—Hanan felt—to avoid going home. Her mother, however, was upstairs and asleep when she came home at 1:00 A.M., and Hanan fumbled with her keys to unlock the door. She woke up late the next morning to the sounds and smells of breakfast being prepared downstairs. She started when she saw her clock read 8:42, but then remembered that it was Satur-day and sank back into the pillows on her bed.

She gazed up at her ceiling as she listened to her mother's and Rola's voices, chatting in Arabic, complemented by an occasional masculine murmur—undoubtedly her father as he watched CNN on the small television in their kitchen. There were tape marks on her ceiling, yellow and brittle, but clinging nevertheless. Back in high school she had taped a poster of Rob Lowe right above her bed so she could fall asleep looking at it. Her mother had denounced it as indecent and ordered her to take it down, but Hanan never did, knowing that it would remain there because her 5 foot 1 inch mother would never reach it, even with a chair, and her father didn't care enough to do something about it himself.

She didn't take it down until she finished high school, when Rob Lowe became as passé as hoop earrings to the shoulder and ultra-feathered hair. But the tape was still stuck to the ceiling—and it struck Hanan that she was a twenty-six-year-old still living with her parents. Should she think about moving out, getting her own place? Maybe that was the jumpstart she needed, to become independent; maybe a small apartment in University City, across the Schuylkill River, like the one John had.

But what about Baba? Hanan imagined him living alone with her mother for the first time in twenty-six years, growing more and more quiet until one day Mama would make a comment about why the garbage disposal was always stopped up and Baba would implode and disappear into a pile of hot ashes.

The sounds in the kitchen quieted when Hanan entered. Her father broke it by glancing up from CNN and saying, "*Sabah al-khair, habibti.*"

"Good morning, Baba," she replied, walking over and kissing his forehead. He smiled absently and raised the volume on the television. Hanan glanced at Rola and her mother as she took a seat at the table. Rola was wearing one of her mother's housedresses, the kind with little, metallic snaps on the bodice sold at K-Mart. She stood by the stove, dropping falafel balls into hot oil, then scooping them out when they were crispy and brown.

"Hanan," her mother said, "we were wondering when you'd wake up." Her unspoken words also registered with Hanan as well: "We were talking and wondering why you left yesterday and where you went." Mama laid plates on the table and a bowl of flat, Arabic bread, two shallow bowls of olive oil and *za'atar* for dipping, as well as a salad of cucumbers, tomatoes, and tahini. Then Rola placed a dish of fresh falafel as the centerpiece of the meal, each one perfectly round and flat, evenly shaped.

"Rola, a friend of mine and I are going to a dance club tonight in the city. Maybe you'd like to come with us?"

"No," Mama said quickly, "Rola has better things to do. She doesn't go to those places."

"'Those places?' Mama, it's not a crackhouse—it's a dance club." She turned her attention back to her cousin. "Want to come? It's a lot of fun."

"No, she doesn't."

"Mama!"

"Yes, I will go."

"Rola!"

"Great!"

"Rola, why do you want to go?" Mama sounded stricken. "You were sick this morning, remember? You are still tired from your trip. These places, they no good! They not for us."

"Mama, you have no idea what you're saying."

"No, *you* don't!" Her mother's words exploded from her lips. "Michel, say something." But her father simply shrugged and returned to the debate on CNN about the foot-and-mouth disease outbreak in England. "Hanan, you are not taking your cousin out tonight. She's from back home—she is not used to these places like you and your friends."

Hanan stood up and took out a Pop-Tart from a box in the cabinet. "I'll skip breakfast—I have to work the noon to eight shift at the store. Besides, I've caused enough trouble in five minutes for the entire day. We'll go around nine o'clock, OK Rola?"

Rola nodded, carefully avoiding her aunt's eyes. Her mother asked if she wanted to make a falafel sandwich, and Hanan shook her head. "See ya." She sailed out of the kitchen, suppressing an urge to smile. Maybe she'd call John later in the afternoon and cajole him into breaking from his thesis and going apartment shopping with her. He'd do anything for a frappacino.

The club was the Eighth Floor, literally on the eighth floor of an old warehouse on the Delaware River. The strip along the river was full of these places that attracted the college students from Drexel and the University of Pennsylvania, the Center City crowd who wore suits in the daytime and miniskirts at night. The club was smoky and dim, with occasional flashing neon pink lights. The DJ stood on a suspended platform with his turntable, overseeing the dance floor, packed with dancing and gyrating and bouncing bodies.

"Do you like it?" Hanan asked, sipping a rum and Coke.

"It's nice," her cousin replied, sipping a plain glass of water. "You come here a lot?" She had a very thick accent, but she spoke English better than Hanan's mother did. Why didn't she speak to her in English before now?, Hanan wondered.

"Yes. My friends and I just come to dance and relax once in a while." She looked over her cousin's outfit and sighed. Rola's jeans were ultra-tight and narrow at the ankles. Hanan had offered to loan her one of her baggy pairs, cinched with a belt. If she'd been stronger in Arabic, she would have told her cousin that tight jeans were the leading cause of yeast infections, but she decided not to even attempt it. She *had* offered to loan Rola some silver jewelry, but Rola had insisted on wearing her heavy gold bracelets, in the 21 karat Arabic style, the kind that Mama had stored away in a safe deposit box for Hanan, "to give you on your wedding day, God willing."

"Your friend? His name is John?"

"Yep."

"He is your boyfriend?"

"No, just a friend. He's really nice. We met in college. I dropped out after the first year, but he stayed on to do graduate work."

"Why did you leave the college?"

"Not for me. I work at a clothing store and spend my time reading, hanging out. We can't all be geniuses."

"Do your parents know that you have a boyfriend?"

"He's not my *boy*friend, Rola. There's a difference," Hanan snapped. There was an awkward silence, until Rola broke it.

"We have clubs in Jordan too, and I went once with my college roommate and her sister. It was fun. Good way to relax before the examinations." She sipped her water. As the light flashed on her thin face, Hanan saw that she was pale and a thin layer of sweat glistened on her upper lip. She looked around nervously, then nearly jumped out of her skin when a young blond man bumped into her. Even Hanan, standing further away, could smell the acrid odor of beer on his breath. He looked at both Rola and Hanan appraisingly, then smiled broadly. Before he could say anything, Hanan said, "Keep moving, pal." He shrugged and, grabbing another beer, moved off into the crowd.

"So you fight with your mother, it seems," said Rola, moving closer to her. Hanan felt suddenly protective of her. "Does it happen very much?"

"Once in a while," said Hanan. "She thinks I should be some perfect Arabic girl, you know, that I should enjoy making cookies and looking for a husband." *Like you*, she thought.

"I know," Rola said sympathetically. "My mother is the same way. Everything I do is wrong, and I don't act the way she wants. I always have to be polite and sweet, even to people I can't stand. Like Uncle Ibrahim." She glanced at Hanan. "You know, of course, he embezzled from the bank he used to manage in Jerusalem? That is why he came to America. He cannot return back!"

"No way! Well, you wanna know what I did to him?" Hanan confessed her story about sticking the bottom of her foot in their uncle's face.

Rola laughed silently, shoulders quivering, then sighed and said, "They are very much a different generation, I am guessing. I should say to you," Rola added in a quiet voice, so soft that Hanan could barely hear her. "I came here thinking that my aunt—your mother— would be different than mine, because she lived here in America. I had hoped . . ." She paused, then shook her head and smiled. "Well, she's more like my own mother than I thought . . . but they are sisters, so it makes sense, of course."

Hanan didn't respond. She felt she needed to sort out this new information. John walked up to them just then, looking weary as usual. "Hello, ladies."

Hanan introduced him to Rola, and before she knew what was happening, John had pulled her surprised cousin onto the dance floor. *Shit*, she thought. This had been their plan, but it just wasn't right anymore. She slammed her glass down onto the bar and hurried after them, cutting through the mass of people like a diver scissoring the water. Rola was trying politely to extricate herself from John, who was pulling her deeper and deeper into the center of the dance floor, like a small ship being sucked into the eye of a swirling, deafening whirlpool.

Hanan called out to John to stop, to call it off, that she didn't want to do this anymore. But the music was louder here, and she felt her whole body vibrate with the noise thumping out of the massive speakers hanging from the rafters above the dance floor.

John was dancing with Rola now, or at least he was dancing, and Rola, jostled by the crowd, was looking around wildly, her hands clasped over her mouth. Hanan reached her just as John stopped, and put a hand on her elbow.

"Rola!" Hanan yelled, "Are you OK?"

Rola shook her head and took her hand away from her mouth long enough to shout, *"Beit al-mai? Beit al-mai?"* She was sweating hard.

"What's that?" John shouted.

"Bathroom," Hanan shouted back. One of the few words she did know. She steered Rola away to the women's bathroom in the back of the hall.

"Everyone out!" she yelled as she barged in the door with her cousin in tow, but there was only one girl standing in the tiny bathroom, applying lipstick in the mirror in front of the two stalls.

"Bitch," the girl muttered, moving away and leaving.

"Just get out!" Hanan moved a trash can in front of the bathroom door. She turned around just in time to see her cousin kneeling before the toilet.

And then of course Hanan knew, and couldn't believe she hadn't understood it before. The sudden decision to come to America, the sickness of her first morning in America. Rola retched for several long minutes, then slumped down on the floor of the stall, looking stunned. Hanan dampened paper towels at the sink and, kneeling beside her, wiped her forehead, her neck and her mouth, and smoothed her hair into place with her other hand. Rola gazed up at her warily, and Hanan was again reminded of how much Rola resembled her mother.

"I need your help," Rola said slowly in Arabic. Hanan understood and nodded.

Later that night, they sat up in Hanan's bedroom, wearing pajamas and drinking hot tea. Mama, glad to see them come home early, had retired for the evening. They formulated a plan together, like conspirators in a plot that could not escape the confines of the room. After they'd settled on most of the details, Rola wept quietly. Hanan wasn't sure if it was from relief or sadness.

"He was in college with me," Rola spoke softly, in Arabic. "We graduated together. I knew it was a mistake but . . . I don't know . . . I was stupid. And then I missed my period."

"What did he say?" asked Hanan in faltering Arabic, the words sounding awkward to her ears, but her cousin did not seem to notice.

Rola folded her arms across her chest, her face white and impenetrable, mummy-like. "He had stopped talking to me by then . . . he ignored me, my calls . . . and then I just got embarrassed because his mother was always the one who answered and I knew that he didn't want to talk to me." She sighed, and said in English, "I felt like such a slut." She pronounced the word more harshly than necessary, hitting the "t" emphatically. "That's what our culture does to you. It makes you feel like a slut for making a mistake."

"American culture does the same thing, believe me. You should hear what some people here still think about single mothers."

"Well, I went back to Ramallah, and all its eyes and ears. And I knew I had to get away, fast, to do this. Hanan," she said, turning to look at her cousin, "it will become apparent in a month or so."

"I know."

"Your mother will tell my mother and my father will never allow me home again. They'll say I disgraced them." She pulled her knees up to her chin and wrapped her slim arms around them. "You're so lucky to live here, Hanan. You don't have to worry about stuff like this. Everything is OK in this country."

"In theory," Hanan said.

"What do you mean?"

"Nothing, really." But she thought of John's little sister, Katrina, who got pregnant in high school. A senior had basically forced it on her. She was expelled, because the school was one of the best private schools in the city and had a reputation to maintain, but the boy wasn't even approached. And she knew that when she eventually took Rola to the clinic, there would be a mob of people there, as there always were, carrying signs and yelling violent slogans. A few of them were quiet, and maintained a sort of dignified vigil, handing out leaflets with options for women, but their voices were drowned out by the others. Hanan passed them every once in a while on her way to work—and it was frightening, perhaps almost as frightening as Rola thought confessing to her parents would be.

Rola dutifully sent an email every few weeks. Stanford was wonderful, she reported, and she was settling in well. She had trouble at first with the language, but thanks to long conversations into the night with John and Hanan during the two months that she remained in

Philly before her semester began, she was able to pick up the idioms and nuances more quickly than she thought. Hanan smiled when she first saw her cousin's email signed, "LOL." *Lots of love to you too,* she thought.

"How's your mother?" she asked Hanan in one email. "Please give her a hug for me."

"Things are better," Hanan had replied, but declined to give more information than that. She had thought of moving out, and had even found a terrific apartment just half a mile away from her job. It would be a great walk in the mornings and evenings, and she could easily hop the subway in bad weather. But her father had looked at her piteously when she mentioned moving out, and her mother had yelled that it was improper for a young girl to live alone, and dangerous in this city, and besides, didn't she care about her parents who had spent twenty-six years slaving to raise her in a good home and provide good food?

But Hanan sensed something behind their attitude, as if they could feel it getting worse. There was something going on, a change in Hanan, and they knew it. She could tell that they thought she'd had enough of them, by the way that she barely stayed home on weekends, or the more and more frequent occasions when she missed dinner with them. "I haven't talked to you in weeks, you stranger," her father said to her jokingly once, but she knew from his twisted, tight half-smile that it was meant to spark a conversation that she did not feel like having just then. And it had been strange indeed, and unnerving, when the clinic had called Hanan to schedule follow-up exams.

"Why is a clinic calling you?" her mother had asked suspiciously. "What is going on?" Hanan had shrugged it off and told Mama not to worry, but of course that did not go over too well. Mama enlisted her father, who came to Hanan one evening after dinner, while her mother had conveniently gone for a walk. "I just wanted to check in with you to see how things are," he said, reaching out as if to pat her hair, but then pulling his arm back as an afterthought. "Is everything OK?"

"Sure, I'm fine," she replied. But that didn't stop the inquiries until Mama confronted her one Saturday morning, when it was her father's turn to conveniently be out of the house.

She stood in the kitchen, her face resolute, but her fingers busy snapping and unsnapping the top button of her housedress. "Hanan," she said, "I know I'm not a too good mother, but I hope you do not do things because you cannot ask me."

Hanan paused from her dishwashing and turned off the faucet. "What are you talking about?" Of course this was about the phone call, but what the hell had her mother mentally conjured up?

"I want to say to you that no matter what you do, I am your mother. I will never be ashamed of what you do or what happens to you. You see?" Mama released her button and spread her fingers out to her sides, palms up, as if to hold up something to Hanan's face. "You are a good daughter. Crazy sometimes, but it's OK. You just have too much energy."

"Thanks." Hanan laughed, and tossed the sponge back into the sink. "But if you're thinking about the phone call from the clinic, that wasn't for me. I was helping a friend of mine out, and she didn't want her parents to know about it."

"Ah, *nushkur Allah!*" But it was a matter of seconds before Mama switched from praising God to asking more questions. "Who was it? I know her?" Mama's eyes flashed curiously, shinier than the metallic buttons on her pink housedress. "Did she come here?"

"Nope, just a girl I work with. You don't know her."

"Well, thank God it was not you. You scare me, Hanan!" Mama still stood in the center of the kitchen, hands outspread. "I think you are feeling alone, and I think is my fault. I know I am too much, but when you really make me mad, and . . . how can I speak the words, Hanan?"

"Yes, yes, I know, Mama." Then, just to keep her mother quiet, to keep the words from coming, Hanan walked over and lifted her in a bear hug, spinning her around the kitchen.

"Crazy girl!" Her mother shrieked, slapping Hanan's back, her plastic slippers sliding off her feet and smacking onto the kitchen floor's tiles. "You are crazy, crazy!" But she did not mention the subject again.

Hanan spent that evening at home, watching CNN with her father and smiling and nodding when he talked animatedly, sometimes to her, sometimes to himself, about the Intifada and Arafat and the refugees still waiting to come home. "How much longer do they have to wait? They are barely holding on to their hopes!" he raged, slamming his fist into the plush armrest of the couch, where it landed without any sound at all. If she did leave, she would miss these oddly distant, but richly familiar moments with him, with this house, even with Mama. In bed that night, she stared at the yellow tape remnants that she couldn't see but that she knew were there. When the sky outside her bedroom window melted from black into a charcoal gray and then slowly into blue, Hanan felt her eyelids falling heavily. The last thing she saw was the tape, still clinging.

Sufficing

Today is Parent's Day at my daughter's school, but I'm not attending. She asked me, last night before she fell asleep, if I could please not go with her. If she could just lie and say that I was sick. She didn't even ask if my feelings would be hurt, but she's only eight and they don't think of these things at this age.

"Why you don't want me to go with you, *albi?*" I asked her, drilling the blanket around her small form, outlining her as a moat does a castle in fairy tales. It makes her feel cozy and sleepy, especially in autumn, when it gets chilly at night. "What's the problem?"

"Because you'll talk differently from the other parents and that'll get me teased for at least a month," she answered casually, then yawned. "OK?"

"OK."

I watch her from the kitchen window now, strolling to the bus stop. Her purple vinyl backpack bumps against the small of her back with each bouncing step she takes. There will be no other children there to wait with her today, because they will all have rides with their parents in their cars. The bus will be empty. Miss Haddon will ask her, "Hanan, where is your mother?" And Hanan will answer in her best grown-up voice, "She is sick today, unfortunately. She could not even get out of bed this morning." She would sit alone at lunchtime and swing by herself during recess, but only to gain the sympathy of the other teachers. The truth is that my daughter usually likes time alone. "I need to think, Mama," she says when I find her sitting on the sofa, with the TV off, just calmly staring at the carpet and swinging her leg back and forth.

I warm the breakfast tea for Michel and me. His employee opened the food cart this morning, so he plans to go in late, in time for the lunch rush. While I keep watch over the kettle, I decide not to tell him about Hanan. He sits at the table, casually reading the newspaper. He likes to read the Ann Landers column, saves it for last, after he's finished with the national and international news. It's like a reward for him. He has been trying to get me to put a television in the kitchen, but I know that he will end up watching it all morning and I only have so much time with him before he leaves.

"Listen to this, *albi*," he says in Arabic, leaning in closer to the page. "This woman's brother-in-law always brings these loose women to their holiday get-togethers, and it doesn't bother anyone else in the family except for her. She wants to tell him to stop bringing these types, but she doesn't want to upset her husband and her in-laws." He chuckles and turns to catch my reaction. "Can you imagine someone back home doing that? It would keep the gossip lines in the village active for years! We'd even hear about it here, across the ocean."

I laugh with him, trying to keep the mood light. I know that he has to leave for work in half an hour, where he'll face lines of customers at the food cart. People in suits and ties and office heels, coming out of office buildings, demanding cheesesteaks with only a "smidgeon" of onions or a soda with "very little" ice. Asking whether or not the meat in the hamburgers is lean and low-fat. Does he have Sweet-n-Low instead of sugar for their coffee? I want to always make these mornings pleasant for him. Just for this small window we rarely have together, between Hanan's departure for school and his own for work.

But he recognizes my uneasiness anyway. He studies my face as I pour the tea for him, the smell of peppermint rising on the clouds of steam, then he pinches my arm gently. "What?"

"Nothing."

"Layla, I know when something is bothering you."

"Hanan's school has Parent's Day today, when the mother or father spends the day with the kids, going to all their classes and meeting their friends and new teachers." I sit down next to him at the table and stir sugar into our teacups. "And she asked me not to come."

He waits for an explanation, so I add, "She's embarrassed about my accent. I felt it from her before, but not like this."

He doesn't know what to say, so he doesn't say anything. This is actually one of the things I love about him. He doesn't prattle and spew empty words and phrases, he just smiles understandingly. Sympathetically. And he squeezes my hand.

But he doesn't comprehend the details, the nuances of my feelings. He was born in the States, raised here, went to school here. He speaks English with a South Philadelphia accent, stretching the last word of every sentence, making it elastic. "Have a nice day now, awh-ight?" or "You want ketchup and muustaard? No praah-blem." I stopped helping him in the cart when Hanan was born, but I still remember.

He married me ten years ago, a girl from the Old Country, because he wanted to keep in touch with his culture. "I'm proud to be an Arab," he said when we were courting. "And I've dated American girls, but they never understand my culture. I think they don't really like it."

I told him that I didn't really understand American culture; I had only arrived a few months before. But I knew that there was an entire pack of Arab-American boys and girls, looking for spouses among us, the newly-landed. I wanted him to love me because I was myself, not because I represented some missing link in his life. But I took a chance on him, and I don't regret it except in moments like this, when I wish I was American enough for my daughter.

He is always kind and eager to please me. We even spent our honeymoon back home in Ramallah, so that I could see my aunts, uncles, cousins, and friends. During those two weeks, I introduced him to the sights and landmarks of a country he'd always heard tales about, but that he'd never experienced. He got upset when I took him to visit the refugee camp where I used to live. His hands shook when he saw the children playing in the open sewers, and the holes, like gaping mouths filled with jagged teeth, that opened the surfaces of many of the homes. "You lived like *that*?" he seethed for days afterwards. But I wanted to show him the good things too, so we went to the Dome of the Rock in Jerusalem, Manger Square in Bethlehem, and the old city of Jericho.

And when we returned to America and settled into our home in Philadelphia, he helped me. We saw the Liberty Bell, or "the bell with the crack," as I reported to my family in my letter home. I also sent pictures of Michel and me in front of the Art Museum, sitting on the big steps. "Michel told me that they filmed a movie here, of a man running up the steps. They made a statue of him later," I wrote. Sometimes, in the summer, we packed a basket and made a picnic by the Delaware River, on the stone benches of Penn's Landing. We paid four dollars each and toured the historic ships anchored in the harbor, ships that hadn't stirred in decades and now suffered visitors crawling inside their bellies. "I used to see all these places when I was a kid, on school trips," he said to me in his still-stilted Arabic (he has improved greatly since then), "but it's different seeing them with you. It's nicer."

I look at him now, at his plump cheeks. Smooth face—he shaved his mustache a week after we married, upon my request, though he still joked that it would return one day. His thick, black hair, which he's never had to color once, even though he's approaching thirty-nine. He's proud of that. A bit relieved, too, because his father and brothers had all been gray at this stage.

I try to be sufficiently Arab, but just American enough for him. It's easy, because small things make him happy. My repeated attempts to fry chicken without burning it. The "A's" I bring home from my ESL classes at the community center. The fact that I've taken to Bruce Springstein (which really was not as tough as I'd made it seem) and listen to Hanan's tapes.

I used to think it would be just as effortless with Hanan.

"I want our children to know their culture. I don't want them to have to find it, like I did," Michel had said. Thus, our firstborn child was given an Arabic name. In first grade, she announced that she hated it.

"Why couldn't I be Laura? Or Miranda?" she asked over dinner one night. "All the kids laugh at my name and the teachers never say it right." It was a logical and practical complaint, but Michel and I agreed in bed that night that we had done the right thing. That this would blow over soon, because it was only her first year in school. Our second child was supposed to have been a boy. We had the name "Kareem" picked out, but we lost him at seven months and never tried again. Since then, Hanan has been my life, despite her reluctance.

Michel leans over me now and kisses my cheek. "I have to run to work, *albi*," he says. "But don't think about Hanan. We knew we'd have problems like this, but it'll pass."

"You think?" I don't want him to leave yet, want to hear his reassurance.

"I went through the same thing she's dealing with now." As if he's read my mind, he hugs me tightly. "She'll get over it." He pours the extra tea in his insulated travel cup and walks out.

The day passes in a frenzied blur. I spend it cleaning the bathrooms and deodorizing the carpets. I should be studying for an English test in a few days but I cannot think. I could also be reading another chapter in my novel. I try to read one every month. This month I am working on a mystery, and usually I can get lost in it, even though I have to pause to look up a lot of the words. But now all I can see is Hanan's face in the semidarkness, sleepily telling me that my accent embarrasses her. I wonder what will embarrass her when she is in junior high school? Will she want a mother who is an executive, who wears powder blue suits and shiny, leather shoes that cost more than our living room furniture? Or a mother who knows all the American music and teaches her to play softball and bake peach pies? Maybe our modest row house in South Philadelphia, with the used dining room set and the worn, burgundy carpets, will not satisfy her. I'm afraid that she'll grimace when I speak to her in Arabic. That she'll answer, pointedly, in English.

I'm afraid that I will not be enough for her.

Hanan comes home from school at 3:30 and I ask her about her day. "Fine," she says, with a shrug. She collects her T-ball equipment, changes into leggings, shorts and her jersey, and hurries out. She yells out a quick goodbye as the door closes. She walks to the field with her girlfriends every day. I imagine them swinging their bats, chattering about when they will graduate from T-ball to "real" baseball, how they will be better than the boys on the team.

I rush to the door, ready to ask her if she wants me to walk her and her friends to the field. But I stop quickly because there is Kristen's mother, pushing the stroller with her newborn baby behind the girls. She sees me and waves, then says something to Hanan, who does not even turn around. Kristen's mother glances back at me sheepishly, offering a feeble and confused smile.

Back home, I would go after Hanan and slap her face. But here, Kristen's mother would call the social services police to come and take my daughter. The only country where disrespect is enforced. I close the door and go back inside.

My hands are shaking and I almost laugh, because the last time someone made me shake like this, he was wearing a helmet and carrying a big black rifle over his shoulder. It was 1967 and I couldn't understand why everyone in Ramallah was fleeing, why the world had suddenly exploded. I was running behind my mother, trying to keep up, knowing I had to because she was holding my brother Ibrahim, whose leg was bleeding. I remember shaking because I didn't want to be left behind, and I didn't know if my father would be up in the cave with my other brothers and my grandmother like he had promised he would be. The soldier fired once again, and my mother fell and pulled me to the ground. *"Uskuti!"* she ordered, and I obediently shut my mouth, making sure the bullet had not hit her or Ibrahim. No, there it was . . . it had made a small hole in the wall behind us. The soldier ran by us, then came back and looked. I screamed and covered my eyes. I heard him laugh, but when I opened my eyes, he was gone.

I walk to the small writing table in the living room, and take out a piece of paper. I write a letter, like I've seen in "Dear Abby." I address it to Hanan, and prop open my grammar book to help me with the tenses and constructions.

> *Dear Hanan,*
>
> *I would like for you to know that you hurt my emotions yesterday and today. Adult people have emotions like children, and we are also available to be hurt . . .*

After I finish it, I fry some chicken for dinner and I don't even burn it that badly—a small accomplishment. I make a *fattoush* salad, with toasted pita bread tossed in like croutons among the lettuce, parsley, tomatoes, and lemon. I stir a pitcher of iced tea, the kind from the can. Hanan hates the homemade, brewed kind. I learned that a long time ago.

I set a small candle on the table, jasmine scented. Hanan and Michel come home usually around the same time, at 6:00, and I'll light it then. I place the letter by her plate, propped up against her pink Barbie glass. My hands are no longer shaking and I hope that my writing will be clear, that she will focus on my meaning, not on the way I unintentionally misspell words or incorrectly conjugate verbs. I hope that she will not look up after reading it and declare that she needs to think, then retreat to her room and swing her leg while shutting me out. I hope that she will not toss my letter casually in her purple and silver wastebasket and wish that I was more like Kristen's mother. I hope that I will be enough.

Costumes

The day my father was robbed was the worst in our lives. "Only so far," my mother warned. "There are always things worse in this life." But this made nobody feel better, not Baba and not me. Actually, this is when I remember first feeling that I hated her.

Baba came home very late that night. We didn't realize how late, though, because it was the night before Halloween. I was leaning, excited, against the kitchen table where Mama had set up her sewing machine. While a tub of okra and tomato sauce simmered, and a pot of peppermint tea lazily boiled on the stove, I attentively watched Mama stitch sequins and ribbons to my costume. I had finally convinced her to let me dress up like Madonna, even though she refused to budge on letting my belly show. My lacy shirt would remain firmly tucked into my long, slim black pants, which would themselves peek through my ruffled babydoll skirt. It was Madonna "on a winter's day," Mama said firmly. But at least she'd promised to let me smudge black liner around my eyes. "Kohl," she nagged. "Your Madonna got that from us." I didn't mind the nagging as long as her hands stayed busy on the machine, finishing off what would be the best costume of any sixth-grader in the neighborhood.

When I heard the doorknob jiggle and the click of the turning key, I rushed to the door, jumping at Baba to get a kiss before Mama beat me to it. His kisses were unparalleled—he would grab the lucky one in a bear hug and plant kisses on her forehead and cheeks, then swing her around the living room, legs barely brushing the coffee table. I always made sure it was me, and Mama had to wait her turn and settle for a demure kiss on the lips.

But he made no move to touch either of us that night, only held up his palms. "Move away from the door," he said. I looked up at him carefully, seeing the cut on his cheek and the dried blood on his cracked lips. He seemed dazed and weary, and I was suddenly frightened deep inside. Behind him was a giant of a man, carrying his hat in his hands and wearing a blue uniform that glittered with badges and pins. His face was pale, and his red hair and white complexion made him look like a corpse, the life and vigor drained out of him, next to Baba, with his disheveled black hair and his skin the color of almond shells.

Mama stood behind me, demanding to know, in her horrible English, what was going on. Baba invited the officer to please sit down, and did he want any coffee? He did not, and I think that was a good thing since Mama seemed unable to make it at that point. She stood, her eyes never leaving our guest, and demanded again to know what happened.

Baba asked me to go upstairs to my room, and I knew better than to argue. His eyes were exhausted, but his hands shook nervously, like he would explode if triggered. I climbed upstairs quickly, but crouched at the top and heard it all—the statement, the story, Mama freaking out, all of it.

Later, when I could see the police officer standing at the front door, I pulled myself back, away from the steps. "Good night, sir, ma'am," he said. "We don't have much to go on, but I'm going to make sure I personally patrol your area. A lot of vendors rent those garages for their carts, don't they?"

"Yeah," Baba said, "and most of us get back to our garages around 7 or 7:30."

"I'll keep closer tabs, then. These guys obviously know the routine—they were waiting for you."

Mama didn't sleep that night—I could hear her sobbing. I think Baba called Auntie Siham, Nadia's mother, to come and stay with her because as I was drifting off to sleep, Mama's strangled voice floated upstairs from the kitchen into my head. "Why did I even come here to this country?" I heard her wail, but that may have been part of my own dreams.

I had to fight with Mama to let me go trick-or-treating the next night. "It's not safe," she finally screamed, ending our conversation by pulling my costume from between the needles of her machine and stuffing it in the kitchen trash can. When she was in the bathroom later, I pulled it out, knocked off the wet tea bags, gritty coffee filters, and slick cucumber skins, shook out the lace and called Nadia. Auntie Siham finally convinced Mama by bringing Nadia over in her Wonder Woman costume, and offering to escort us around the neighborhood herself. Mama relented, but Auntie Siham had to bring me home by 8 P.M. anyway.

"I heard about your dad," Nadia said. "That's really scary. Do you know what happened?"

"No," I lied. "They won't tell me. All they said is two guys stole money from my dad when he was in his garage." We were strolling from row house to row house, ringing the doorbells of only those with their lights on. Auntie Siham stayed on the sidewalk behind us, pulling her gray coat tightly around her, the wind whipping her silky black hair around her face. I loved Nadia's mother—she was always cool and stylish, serving baklava in tiny, pink plates and juice in matching pink glasses whenever I visited. She was so unlike Mama, who always seemed frantic about something, who walked around muttering to herself and embarrassed me whenever I had friends over.

"My mom is completely losing it," I said. "She told me I can't go out by myself again, ever."

"I know. My mom was at your house pretty late last night."

So I hadn't dreamed that part. But what about the image of Baba's body, riddled with bullets lying beside his aluminum cart? Of masked men crouching behind my closet door under my bed? Of screaming out for Baba but not being rescued?

Auntie Siham had invited Mama to walk with us, saying the cold air would clear her mind, but she stayed home anyway with Baba, who'd been with her all day long. When I woke up that morning and came downstairs, they were huddled on the couch with their coffee cups, sharing an afghan that was draped over them both. When I left to trick-and-treat, they had moved to the kitchen table, still drinking coffee, not talking much, just staring down at their hands or up at the ceiling. Baba had stayed home from the city that day, because it was a Saturday. He only worked on the cart from Monday through Friday, taking orders for hot dogs, sandwiches, cheesesteaks, and hamburgers, even on the coldest days when the rain hammered down and the wind rattled his aluminum cart, the one with the green, foldout awning, that he hitched to the back of our car and drove to the corner of 16th and Market five days a week.

I'd visited him once with Mama, when he first got the cart. He worked such long hours, leaving the house at 5 A.M. and returning late, that the two of us hardly saw him at all. I had a school holiday, so we decided to spend it seeing Baba in the daylight hours for a change. It took us almost an hour between walking to the subway station, waiting for the train, and then walking the three blocks to the corner where he worked. I remember marveling at how beautiful Center City looked, only a few blocks north of where we lived, but a different world entirely. We'd stood on the sidewalk, waiting to talk to him, but he had a dozen people in line, all in suits, checking their watches, calling out "Hold the mayo" and "Easy on the onions." Baba finally blew us both kisses and opened his hands wide, apologetically, before wrapping a hot cheesesteak, dripping with fried onions, in aluminum foil. We walked back dejectedly toward the subway station, both of us too intensely disappointed to speak to one another on the ride home.

I love my mother. Very much, actually. But she doesn't comfort me the way Auntie Siham comforts Nadia when she fails a test or falls off her bike. Baba doesn't either, but that's not his fault. He's not really around. I guess I don't really rely on Mama too much, although she depends on us pretty heavily. If we're unhappy, so is she. If we don't smile at her every second, if she catches us in the middle of a thought or a concern, she thinks we're mad and she gets upset, slamming cabinet doors and banging glasses down on the table. Once I came home with a "B" on a math test, thrilled really, since I'd struggled with fractions all quarter long. I remember Baba hugged me and gave me $5, and then I suppose I ran right up to my room to hoard it in my money box, forgetting to get a hug from Mama too. The rest of the evening, she muttered angrily about "appreciation" and "respect." And she wouldn't believe I hadn't meant it. When I don't finish my plate at dinner, she lectures me about the refugee camp again, about her life before Baba, about how she and her sisters had to walk to the next village, and knock on the doors of the convent and ask for food. "We would have walked to Bethlehem if we had to!" she says, as if I have any clue where Bethlehem even is and how far it is from where she used to live. Nadia speaks Arabic well and she knows more about "back home" than I do, but I'm a lost cause. My mother has never shown me a map, and I've heard these stories a million times, but she tells them like they are new, as if the memory just popped into her mind and she is living it again.

Sometimes I feel like Baba wants to explain things to me, to tell me something about Mama he thinks I should know. The words form, he leans in, then hesitates and pulls away.

We returned from trick-or-treating at 8 P.M. on the dot, and Mama was smoking a cigarette on our stoop, tapping her foot on the marble steps. She didn't see us approach at first, her eyes fixed on the cement slab of the sidewalk, smoke pouring from her lips like a chimney, the red ash of her cigarette tip a beacon in the dim light. A little boy dressed like the Incredible Hulk approached her and said "trick or treat," but hurried back to his mother when Mama stared right through him.

Auntie Siham went up and put her arm around Mama's shoulders. Nadia and I stayed behind on the sidewalk.

"Layla?"

Mama looked up at her, as if not recognizing her. Then she said, her voice vibrating with tiny tremors, "I thought I would be safe here. He promised I would. Don't you see? He *promised*."

Things changed quickly after the robbery. Nobody told me why, except that we needed to be more careful in general. I no longer went over my friends' houses, and could only play with the other Arab and Palestinian girls in the neighborhood. Nadia introduced me to Reema and Aliyah, who lived only a few blocks away with their families. The three of them became my only friends. Almost every day after school and almost certainly on the weekends, I would pack my music cassettes in a grocery store bag and visit one of them, usually Nadia, the only one of us with a cassette player in her room.

We would shut the door, pick a tape, assign roles, and design a routine. Reema was usually the lead, because she had the best twists and turns, and the rest of us were back-up dancers. I tried to convince them that we should hit the road after high school and join the Solid Gold dancers. "We'd show them some real moves," I claimed one afternoon at Aliyah's house, as we took a break from our routine. We'd kicked her brothers out of the room they all shared, but they'd stationed themselves outside her door with waterguns, ready to jump at us as soon as we ventured out. Nadia's portable cassette player was on the dresser, and the three beds pushed up against the wall. The room was toward the back of the row house, looking over the back alley of her block.

"I won't be allowed to do that," Aliyah said, sucking on a bottle of lemon Gatorade. "I have to go to college—that's what my mom said."

"My mom too," said Reema, undoing and rebraiding her long, thick hair. Her mother has never allowed Reema's hair to be cut since she was born, and it hangs below her hips now. It's the reason why her turns are the best, because her long hair trails after her, dramatizing her moves. "I have to get a scholarship, " she said, "or else."

"Or else what?" I asked.

Reema paused, thinking. "I'm not sure."

"What about you?" I asked Nadia. "Do you need to go to college?"

"Yeah. I have to be a doctor like my grandfather. Or I could marry one—my mom said either one is fine."

"That totally sucks ass," I blurted out. "Why the hell do we spend all our time practicing if we're not going to *do* anything with it?"

They all stared at me, their mouths gaping.

"Hanan, you're gonna get us in trouble," Aliyah whispered fiercely, pressing her ear to the door. "What if my brothers heard you? They'll tell my mom."

"Yeah, Hanan," agreed Reema.

"My mom said she won't let me hang anymore with you if you say stuff like that," Aliyah added.

"You *tell* her what I say?" I shook my head, angrily, pulling my Madonna tape out of Nadia's portable cassette player. They got on my nerves sometimes—they were all proper and dainty, like brown-haired Barbies in pink ruffled gowns, even though their dads didn't make that much more than mine. Like they didn't curse in their heads? I was just more honest because I let it out of my mouth. I started to leave, bracing myself to face the blast of waterguns, but Nadia stopped me and told us all to just forget it.

"Let's get back to practice," she said. And we did. She's like that—always smoothing things over, lightly, easily. Aliyah pulled on a strand of my hair and Reema pretended to tickle me—all signs of making up.

I didn't want to fight anyway. I liked the Palestinian girls in our neighborhood, and they were the only friends I was allowed to see after school anyway. Mama had stopped trusting anyone who was American, anyone who could possibly be a criminal. "At least with the other Arab kids you are safe because their families watch out for you," she said. She had started to spend more time with their mothers too, going with me to visit. The moms played cards and drank coffee while we watched TV, listened to Bon Jovi, and choreographed our dances. Mama seemed happier when we left than when we arrived, smiling to herself as we walked home, sometimes even stopping to let me buy Twizzlers at Dino's Candy "Shoppe"—my favorite store because of the weird spelling and because Mrs. Dino, who slumped behind the counter, glued to her stool and scratching her scruffy mustache, let me sample the jellyfish candies whenever I came in.

"Siham's friends are nice—I'm glad we got to know them," Mama said once on the way home. "It feels good to have your own people around you."

"Are you still scared, Mama?" I asked her, pulling apart the red braids of my candy.

"We have to always be scared, Hanan," she replied.

"I hate you," I said inside my head, wanting to scream it to the whole neighborhood, so loud that Mrs. Dino would fall right off her stool, because my mother wanted me to feel as helpless as she did.

The day before Thanksgiving, Mama sent Baba to the Colonial Village grocery store to buy a fresh turkey. She had invited Reema's, Nadia's, and Aliyah's families—a total of about eighteen people, including us—for dinner. She had never cooked a turkey before, but Aunt Siham loaned her the recipe and her turkey roasting pan.

She asked me to stay with her to chop potatoes, but I said I was going with Baba. "I need your help here!" she yelled, but Baba stepped in and told her we wouldn't be long at all. We both scurried out before she could think of an argument.

He looped an arm around my shoulders as we walked, but removed it to make the sign of the cross as we passed the St. Nicholas of Tolentine Church on 9th Street. I'd never seen him do that before, not once in the dozens of times we had walked the eight blocks to Colonial Village and passed the somber, gray-stone church. But I instinctively crossed myself too, just because he had.

"Why did you do that?" I asked, tugging on his arm.

"Why not?"

"Baba, c'mon. How come? You never did that before."

He ignored me, and we continued quietly side-by-side, past the Dominican hair salon, past the Lebanese café, where Baba waved to the slim, mustached man behind the counter, past the Italian bakery, where the smell of fresh bread and pastries stirred my appetite. "They're baking cannolis in there," I hinted.

"On the way back," he promised. "First, the turkey."

But in the refrigerated meat department in the rear of the store, his face blanched as he watched the butcher wrap the headless bird in plastic, and I thought he would faint at the sight of the other butcher, trimming the fat off blocks of red meat, bright blood smeared over his white apron.

"Seeing that blood freaked me out," he confessed on the way home, as we lugged the turkey back, each of us grasping one of the plastic bag's handles. "It made me sick to my stomach."

I didn't think anything ever freaked Baba out, not even when he'd almost lost his own finger putting an air conditioner in the living room window. He actually had scars all over his hands, the result of working in a cart where you had to chop steaks all morning to have them ready to grill by lunchtime. That had never made him sick to his stomach. And what about the time a police car jumped the curb and slammed into his cart? Hot grease had splashed on his face and the whole cart had slammed to the ground. One broken collarbone—had that scared him? I doubted it—I doubted anything could scare him, until now.

I remembered what I'd heard that night, crouching at the top of the staircase. Heard Baba making his statement to the police—how the two men, wearing masks, had leapt out of the dark corners of his garage as soon as he'd pulled in his cart and rolled down the door behind him. How they had forced him down on his knees, hands behind his head, as they broke open the locked, aluminum box that he kept on the top shelf of the cart. How the cold steel of a gun had been pressed against the side of his head, how he had begged for his life, pleading that he had a wife and a little girl who needed her father. How the triggerman finally relented, despite his partner's protests to just "shoot the motherfucker," and how a kick to the stomach and a blow to the side of the head had satisfied them. Baba had seen them creep out the door, the blood oozing into his eyes, before he'd passed out. That had done it. Now he would always be afraid. I imagined him slowly morphing into Mama, and wondered if I had to start hating him a little too.

We passed the bakery, and he forgot about the cannolis, and I didn't ask. But when we passed the church and he crossed himself again, I made a point not to. I'd help myself from now on.

The Journey Home

The day I married John, my mother was at home, venting her anger by smoking cigarettes and watching the clichéd and overly dramatic Arabic soap operas on the satellite TV. "I will not give you my blessing—never!" she'd said when I came home with a small diamond on my finger and John on my arm. "What do you want with an *amerkani*?"

So she stayed stubbornly home that day, while I recited my vows to a beaming John, at the St. Nicholas Catholic Church. Though the church was right around the corner from my parents' house, no amount of cajoling from anyone would make her accept this marriage. Maybe it really was because John was an *amerkani*, or, more likely, because I was pregnant.

Aliyah and Reema were there, both wearing the black and white bridesmaid dresses I'd picked out. Nadia was not there, but that was expected. And Baba was there, of course. I'd known he would come through for me. Even during the terrible weeks and months before the ceremony, when Mama's yelling drove me out of their house and into John's apartment, Baba would smile at me in the darkest moments, a quick, soft smile behind Mama's retreating back as she thumped up the steps. Even while doors slammed and Mama screeched, "You are always making trouble, *ya* Hanan!"—even then, I did not doubt Baba would escort me down the aisle and kiss my cheek when we reached the altar.

He did just that—and then he turned to John and shook his hand firmly. "You are my son now." That sent Aliyah and Reema into a flash of tears. Me too, although I blinked valiantly to fight them because of my expensive makeup job.

After the priest, old and wrinkled Father Anthony, declared us husband and wife, John and I flew down the aisle—past Baba's smiling face, past Reema's and Aliyah's joyful weeping, and past the clapping of our fifty guests—back to the marbled foyer of the church.

"Hey Mrs.," John said, pulling me into his arms.

I giggled excitedly. "This is so fantastic—it's perfect."

"Yeah?" He looked down, searchingly, into my face. "Even without your mom here?"

"It's perfect," I repeated clearly, emphatically, so that neither of us would forget that I meant it.

The house John and I bought was in University City, on 38th Street, nestled behind the University of Pennsylvania campus. It was an older town house that cost much more than we could afford, but John's parents had made the down payment as a wedding gift. Three floors high, it had polished hardwood floors, curved banisters, cathedral-style windows, and a stone balcony overlooking the back of the house.

Our home, the one with the dark red front door, had a small backyard with thick green grass that John said I'll love until I had to mow it in the summertime. I'd never mown grass before, but I doubted I'd mind. It had to be better than sweeping off the cement block that served as the backyard of my parents' row house pushing the debris and stepped-on cockroaches into the back alley. I hated that backyard, ever since I was a little kid.

One year, in fourth grade probably, I became fixated on the idea of a pool. The kids on the TV shows I used to watch usually had one, a dark blue one with fake wood paneling that rose from the ground in their lush green backyard. It was almost June, but already the humidity was creeping through the back alleyway and into the homes of everyone in the city. Mama flapped out white sheets on the carpet of the living room, because without an air conditioner, that was the coolest room in the house. The worst feeling was walking up to my room in the morning to get dressed for those last, hazy days of school and feeling like a blanket was dropping down on me, smothering me more tightly with each step upward.

And so I wanted a pool, to swim up and break through the surface of clean, cold water, grinning madly and tossing a volleyball to my brothers and sisters. I didn't have any brothers or sisters, of course. Mama never wanted to give me a straight answer when I asked why I was the only one. But a pool was do-able, a real possibility.

Mama resisted. "How can we put a pool like that in this yard?" she beseeched me. "The pool would be bigger than the yard, and would you bring the water to fill it?" I was nine and didn't care, and so I sulked for weeks, pushing Mama's food on my plate without eating it and not talking to her when she asked me how school was or if I needed my uniform shirt pressed.

And then one day, after June had started and the end of the school year was only days away, Mama grinned at me when I walked in the door at 3:30 P.M. Throwing my purple vinyl backpack on the armchair by the door, I raced through the dining room, past the kitchen and out the backdoor. And there it was, a pink plastic tub, about six inches deep, filled with water, with Barbie's face swimming up from its shallow depths.

I went back inside, back to the chair, grabbed my backpack, and climbed up to my room. Mama stood uncertainly at my door, but I just told her I wanted to be alone. The air in my room was thick and sticky, but I stayed in it, sweating and shedding miserable tears, until it was time for dinner. A week later, I saw the pool in Nadia's back-yard, behind the flower shop, a shallow pink circle on her own ce-mented slab.

John had claimed the second-floor guest bedroom as his office, leaving me a corner of the basement for my crafts room. While he had a door to close on himself, to lock him inside with his wall of soci-ology books and his computer and writing table, my supply of paints, wooden strips, and threads had to settle for a utility table on the brown linoleum floor. The only television in the house was down here too, but I rarely watched any of it. I enjoyed making gift baskets, and TV only distracted me. I liked to make these baskets for the house, for friends. When Aliyah got her own apartment in Center City two years ago, I made baskets for every room in the place. In this new house, I planned to do the same: one basket in almost every room. My parents' house was also filled with these baskets, which my mother used to make by weaving strips of olive branch wood, soaked in paint, into round or flat shapes. First she built a foundation, then the sides, and finally she weaved in other strips as a decorative pat-tern. "In the camp, a UNRWA program come and tell us, do this and we give you money," she said, "so we do it." Her mother and aunts had done it for years, and though my mother didn't particularly enjoy it, she had discovered that she could make money by weaving these designs.

I wanted to stamp every room in the new house with my impres-sion, to mark it for myself. Our furniture belonged to John, the heavy oak coffee table and the sofas in the blue plaid pattern that were do-nations from his grandfather. They still smelled like Pops Martin—I breathed in the scent of cigar smoke and Old Spice whenever I napped on one of them, waiting for John to come home from teaching his class at the university. Teaching sociology 101 and other basic courses were part of his assignments as an instructor at Drexel Uni-versity. "I need to prove myself, sweetie," he explained to me once, "not by my teaching—that means nothing, really. I have to write books, give conference papers, prove myself that way." He wanted a tenure-track position, and it was all part of publish or perish, he told me. I loved how smart John was—I'd met him in college, when he was even skinnier than he was now, though he still wore the same pair of old-fashioned, horn-rimmed antique glasses. His brown hair still had the same sheen, thickness, and curl, and I enjoyed sitting with him in front of our small black cast-iron stove, running my fingers through his hair as he lay his head in my lap, talking and watching the logs burn.

"How do you like our house?" he asked me lazily one night. It was three months after the wedding, and we'd just painted the upstairs guest room a soft, green color. It would be the nursery and we wanted to avoid pinks and blues.

Since the wedding, I had felt like we lived on our own island, in our small house in University City, far from South Philly where my friends lived. Where Mama and Baba lived. Mama and I had not spoken or seen each other, except for a few tense telephone calls when I'd tried to check on Baba, who was feeling sick more and more often.

"I love our house," I replied to John, gently lifting his head off my lap and stretching out beside him on the rug. "I've gotten used to it."

"But it's a longer commute to your job, right?"

"Sure," I answered, "but I can always find something closer." I worked at a clothing store on Passyunk Avenue, next to an Italian bakery and a furniture store that had both been there forever. I remember, as a kid, spending half of my $1 weekly allowance on a vanilla-cream topped cupcake with colored sprinkles, eating it in front of the furniture store window while dreaming about the kind of furniture I would have in my own home some day.

"Why don't you think about finishing your degree instead of working?" John said.

I remained quiet, then said, "Maybe soon, but not now. Not until after the baby comes."

We didn't speak for a while, but then he continued, "Why don't we have your parents over for dinner soon?"

I looked at him in such a way that he became quiet. "You know I'm not supposed to get stressed out."

"You need to reconcile with your mother, Hanan," he pressed me. "It's the only way to become a successful mother yourself."

On our first night in the house, our wedding night, we made love on a quilt on the bedroom floor. The king-size bed we'd ordered hadn't come in yet, and no other room in the house seemed right enough. Afterwards I stayed awake, rubbing gently at the discomfort in my belly, where the skin was already becoming taut. I was thinking how good it felt to lie in John's arms, my head nestled in the triangle of his shoulder, arm, and chest—a soft, fleshy spot that became a pillow for my cheek. It felt nice to know that I didn't have to rush home to my parents' house, where, whenever my car pulled up in front, the curtains of the front window would slightly waver, and I knew Mama had been waiting there. After I had moved in temporarily with Aliyah, she would call me loyally whenever I slept at John's. "Your mom's been calling all night," she'd say. And I'd race to the apartment early, before dawn, and pull on my pajamas because, sure enough, Mama would be there by 7:00 A.M. to surprise me.

"What are you talking about, Mama?" I asked once, sleepily rubbing my eyes. I had sped home, maneuvering through the snow that had fallen the night before. "Of course I've been here all night."

"Then why did Aliyah said she doesn't know where you are when I call?" She faced me like a war general, her hands in fists on her hips, her handbag slinging from her forearm, her eyes—even without kohl—still fierce and black.

"I came home when Aliyah was asleep, and she didn't know I was there when you called and woke her up." I moved into the kitchen, and Mama followed me closely, like a predator thinking her prey would take flight and escape. "Right, Aliyah?"

Poor Aliyah stood by the kitchen table, wiping it off so she could lay down her notebook and write. "Yes, Auntie," she lied smoothly, though I didn't miss the sharp look she threw in my direction. "I didn't know Hanan was home."

There was a slight pause, and I knew my mother realized I had won. There was no way she would ever accuse Aliyah, her friend's daughter, of lying, and because of that, I could relax. "Coffee, anyone?" I asked, pulling a coffee filter from the stack in the cupboard. "I'll make a pot."

"I'll have a cup," Aliyah murmured, sharpening her pencils over the wastebasket.

"American coffee?" Mama asked, opening the freezer door. "I thought I—yes, here it is," she said. She pulled out a bag of Arabic ground coffee and switching to Arabic, added, "You girls forget everything when you live away from your families."

She took the pot of water I was about to pour into the machine and poured it instead into a narrow but deep frying pan we had. "Next time, I will bring one of my Arabic coffee pots, the one with the long handle. That American coffee tastes like dirty water."

After it had boiled, Mama stirred in sugar and cardamom, which she pulled from a plastic bag in her purse. She kept everything from peppermint candies to individual aspirin pills to mint leaves in plastic bags in her bag, because she had a phobia about being unprepared. She often called Ziploc bags the best invention of the twentieth century. We took our cups to the living room, leaving Aliyah alone so she could write. Mama sat on the armchair and I on a large, embroidered floor pillow that Aliyah's mom, Aunt Lamis to her friends' children, had stitched for the apartment.

"I know you like living here," Mama said in Arabic, "and you and Aliyah must feel like you have so much freedom in your lives now."

"That's exactly how we feel," I answered in English.

She noted my answer, but persisted in Arabic, her lips hissing around every letter. "Neither your Auntie Lamis nor I are happy with this arrangement. It's just not right, Hanan."

I didn't want to continue the conversation, so I stayed quiet. That is my usual strategy, developed when I was a teenager and had to argue about every outfit or hair style I wanted to wear outside the house. We'd had this talk so often during the month before I moved out, I felt I could lecture myself.

"Hanan," she continued, "it's been three months now. Why don't you come home? Your father misses you."

"Don't put Baba into this, Mama," I warned. I should have anticipated this move.

I could tell by her face that she was hedging, envisioning her next approach. "And me, Hanan? I can't stand what people are saying about you and Aliyah. I know it not true, but they poison people's minds. And Lamis," she added, lowering her voice, "already thinks you the one who convinced Aliyah to get her own apartment in the first place."

"I don't care what they're saying. Just ignore it. I'm not going to spend my whole life worrying about what Lamis and everyone else thinks of me."

"I know—I should tell them go tile the ocean. But it's not so easy for me. You don't care how people look at me. Old Mrs. Samara in the pharmacy last week ask me how you are. And such a look on her face! I grab your father's medicine and leave so fast, without answering her."

I sipped the last of my coffee, and turned the cup upside down on the saucer. "Want to read my cup?" I asked, trying to change the subject. "The grounds will dry soon."

A flush spread slowly over her cheeks, maroon blotches on her olive skin. "No, thanks," she answered. "I can see your future without looking in your cup."

As I lay with John on our first night as a married couple, I remembered that had been one of the last times she had visited the apartment, because soon after, I announced my engagement.

A few weeks after the wedding, I was at work, dressing my mannequin in the window. Her head was busted and taped up in the back, making it difficult to pull the tight red turtleneck over it and down her torso. I struggled with her for a while, even tilting her sideways to maneuver the clothing over her slim frame, but I was having no luck and had only worked up an intense sweat. It was when I had ripped the denim skirt off the mannequin and given up on the turtleneck altogether, and was standing there with the nude foam and plastic figure, deciding what to do, that I noticed John's mother walking by, carrying her groceries in eco-friendly canvas totes. She only came down to South Philly to shop at Zagarella's Italian grocery store, because all her friends shopped there. "They make their own pasta," she told me once, which explained why she made the twenty-minute trip.

I banged on the window until she turned around, bags dangling on both her sides, her heavy crocheted purse hanging from her shoulder.

John's mother had a soft face, which rolled up into a gentle smile when she saw me. Her hair was, as usual, coiled up into a tight twist, although small wisps of steel gray framed her forehead, smoothing the otherwise harsh style. Her eyes, like John's, shone dark blue, like sapphires.

I hurried out to the front door to see her. She returned my hug gently. "Don't want to hug you too hard," she said with a small laugh, gesturing toward the bulge at my belly. "How are you, Hunan?" She still pronounced my name like it was a region of China, but I had given up trying to correct her.

"Fine, Mom," I answered. "You're doing your shopping early this morning, huh?"

"John's uncle is coming for dinner tonight. Why don't you and John and your parents join us, dear?"

"My parents are busy, I think. But maybe John and I will stop by, if we don't have to attend a dinner his department is hosting." I hoped we didn't have to go, because I really didn't like John's colleagues.

"Alright," she answered, then she looked startled as she glanced into the store window. "Oh my, your mannequin is missing her clothing—and part of her head!"

"Sorry," I said, unsure of what I was really apologizing for. "I need to get her and some others into new spring outfits."

"Are you still planning to stay here, at this job, Hunan?" she asked. "In this little place?"

"Yes, at least until I have the baby. Why?"

"Oh. Well. I thought John said you were planning to go back to school soon."

I shook my head. "I said I was thinking about it, Mom."

"Well, perhaps I misunderstood," she said diplomatically.

When she had walked away, her canvas totes bumping against her legs, I returned inside and stood in the window, gazing out onto Passyunk Avenue. The message had been delivered.

The street hummed and clicked with sounds of the old Italian women picking up their bread at the bakery and the girls in their plaid skirts and saddle shoes, walking to St. Maria Goretti High School, which I had also attended, even though our uniforms back then had been much uglier. I watched them walk by every morning, laughing on the way, while I tagged shirts with sale stickers and aligned handbags on the shelves, putting the store in order before it was time to open for the day's business. They probably arrived in homeroom by 8:30 A.M., and then spent the day being told, as I had been, that they could achieve anything. My friend Aliyah had heeded that message—her writing career was blossoming. Nadia, who nobody had thought would do anything more than eventually get married to George and have some kids, had surprised us all as well. Nobody knew why she'd broken off their relationship, but George was becoming a ghost, haunting me, Aliyah, and Reema for clues, for some hope. It was tragic to watch.

Even Reema had attended Goretti with us. Jewish girls also went to Goretti, and like them, Reema had to sit through classes on Catholicism. Maybe she thought she had something to prove, but she got A's in that class and in all her other courses. She was finishing a PhD in sociology at the University of Pennsylvania, where John had finished his own degree.

I thought about Mrs. Martin's face when she realized I still worked at Lucia's and planned to stay for a while. Her bright blue eyes had disclosed a brief flash of pity.

I met John's parents long before he met mine. They were both teachers, she a history teacher at the archrival of the high school I had attended, and he a biology teacher at the Community College of Philadelphia. They both hailed originally from northeast Philly, part of the entrenched Irish community, but moved to Center City in the early '70s. I know they didn't really like South Philly, maybe because of the immigrant communities that turned street corners into gathering places and where a row home often housed four families. South Philly consisted of a steady stream of Irish who hadn't ever stopped arriving, even decades after the potato famine; the Italians, mostly from Sicily, who invariably set up pizzerias, selling tomato pies they never consumed at home but which they learned was apparently very Italian; the Vietnamese, who pooled together the money of several families and bought and managed Chinese food shops and restaurants, because nobody seemed to notice the difference and because most people still felt pissed about the war.

"So I guess my parents are stereotypically boring people," John told me one night at the used bookstore on South Street, where we used to meet. It was the night I was going to meet his parents, and he wanted to fill in the background of details, the context of how he came to be. "So they may be curious and ask you lots of questions because you're ethnic . . ."

I stifled a laugh. I couldn't help it.

"What's so funny?"

"I just hate that word. 'Ethnic.'"

"It's a fine word," he said defensively.

He asked if I wanted to go now, since his mother was making dinner at six o'clock. But I preferred to stay a while longer at the bookstore, just a few more minutes to brace myself. John said, "Sure," and headed up to the second floor to check out the sociology books. He could read a book in just a few days, or even several hours, which amazed me. I'd decided to drop out of college soon after I got an "F" on an English Composition 102 paper. The instructor, who was just a teaching assistant anyway, wrote something like "Poor organization" or "Doesn't address the point of the assignment." Of course it didn't, because I never understood the goddamn assignment in the first place. How should I know or care to know how to write a comparison and contrast of two poems? Of Robert Frost, no less? "Swinger of Birches," my ass. In Philly we called trees "trees"—just that. Nothing more specific beyond that because there were not enough of them populating the streets to warrant naming them individually. A tree, growing fragilely out of a square of uncemented sidewalk, is just a tree.

John and I drove to Chestnut Street. His parents lived just north of Rittenhouse Square, a neighborhood that made me feel like a phony. We parked his car and held hands on the way over to their town house. Cast-iron troughs, filled with fresh flowers, lined the two windows on the first floor, and each set of three windows on both the second and third opened out onto a narrow, cast-iron balcony. The front steps were polished marble, and the front door was made of dark wood with black trim. It opened as we climbed the steps, and his mother, wearing a pale green spring dress with low-heeled espadrilles, greeted us.

"You must be Hunan."

The day I told John I was pregnant—a month before our wedding— reminded me of the day I met him. I was waiting for Reema at the base of the Ben Franklin statue on Locust Walk, on the University of Pennsylvania campus. It always felt weird on campus because I never looked like the other students. The other girls dressed like Reema and Aliyah—they wore long, corduroy pants that hung in straight lines from their hips, and thick, knarled yarn socks in luggish, brown leather sandals. They never wore close-fitting jeans that showed their curves, while I did—and I liked to wear the black leather boots that I'd spent a week's salary on.

So there I stood, waiting, thinking that maybe it was time to quit college. I couldn't believe I'd gotten into the University of Pennsylvania, anyway—my grades in school were always very good, but the only reason I could afford it was that Federal Aid leaped to the rescue. "But," I asked Ben Franklin silently, staring at his wrinkled face, "did I want to spend the next thirty years paying back student loans for an experience I didn't love in the least? Maybe this place you founded isn't for everyone."

Reema approached, strolling toward me in her Birkenstocks and a baggy white fisherman's cable-knit sweater, her hair tied up in a haphazard bun. A backpack, bursting with books and papers, decorated her back like a camel's hump. She smiled and waved.

As she came closer, I started to say "hi," but Reema was intercepted by a tall guy with brown hair and bright blue eyes, who started talking to her without even acknowledging me. Reema smiled again, apologetically, this time at me. He was chattering about some class they had together, about a homework assignment he didn't understand.

I tapped him on the shoulder. "Excuse me, I think I was here first."

He turned and looked down at me, his bright blue eyes squinting at me in the glaring autumn sun, his curly brown hair tousled by the wind, his broad shoulders shaking to readjust the weight of his monstrous book bag across his back in an elegant move.

I wasn't impressed.

"John, this is my friend Hanan," Reema said, laughing, smoothing over the situation. He shook my hand, and I noticed the golden hairs on the back of his hand, in little, square patches on his long fingers, right above the knuckles. "Hi, Hanan," he said, hitting the "H" just right. "You claim to have had a previous appointment with the queen here?"

"Yes, and I've been waiting for ten minutes, since 1:30 P.M., for an audience." He looked surprised, then laughed delightedly.

When I told John I was pregnant, four years later, he was standing in his kitchen, slicing onions to be thrown into the steaming wok on the stove. Lined up on the counter beside him were the next victims waiting to fall under his knife: a bag of string beans, a tomato, and three carrots. Chunks of chicken were already browning in the wok, simmering in a sea of ginger and fragrant oil.

He heard me come out of the bathroom and asked over his shoulder if I could start the rice. "The brown rice—there's a new bag—in the cabinet under the microwave."

"John, I need to talk to you."

"Just a sec, love—let me finish this onion." His hand continued chopping at its same steady pace, not increasing despite the urgency I felt inside of me.

I tapped him on the shoulder. "John, we're going to have a baby."

He turned quickly, spinning like a top, the knife at his side pointed at me. Peering down at me with those intense eyes, he commanded, "Say that again."

"I'm pregnant," I said impatiently. "I just took a test, and it turned blue. I'll have to go to the doctor, of course, but I'm pretty sure . . ."

Tossing his knife into the sink, he carefully rinsed and dried his hands before placing them on my cheeks. "Are you okay with this?"

"Yes. Are you?"

"This is really good news." He kissed me tenderly.

"Good," I said, patting his chest. I went to the cabinet and pulled out a bag of brown rice. "Now we need to plan a wedding."

I went home from work at 3:30, the time that the other assistant manager, Beth, came to fill in. That was another advantage to my job: even though I started my day at 7:30 A.M., an hour earlier than most people, I got home earlier than most of them, too. There was nothing more relaxing than getting home the same time as most school kids, slipping back into my pajamas, boiling a pot of herbal tea, and curling up in a chair with a book or magazine to wait for John.

My stomach cramped up as I sat on the couch in our home, and I carefully set down my cup of tea and rubbed the left side of my belly with the palm of my hand. That was where the baby's head was, the doctor had said. I was only five months along, and of course, this baby wasn't completely developed (not according to *What to Expect When You're Expecting*, which Nadia had bought for me), but I imagined a perfect, miniature human sucking its thumb as it slept in my belly, comforted and lulled by the rhythm of my heartbeat.

For some reason, I started thinking about John's mother, and what she'd said that morning. Why did it bother me so much? Mrs. Martin had never treated me condescendingly—she'd always been kind to me, even when it was painfully clear that I didn't fit in with the Martin family. Once, at Thanksgiving, when John and I were still "just friends," I had picked a chicken leg—with my fingers, not noticing the tongs—from the tray and put it onto my plate, because that was how we did it at home. The dinner table got *real* quiet, as all eyes watched me. Everyone that night took chicken from the opposite side of the tray, leaving a small pile of chicken wings and legs near what I'd touched, like a contaminated leper colony. What would they do if they knew we ate *mansaff* with our hands, rolling the rice and meat into little clumps and popping them into our mouths? For the entire evening, I was known as "Hunan"—or even "Huran" by one elderly aunt who wore fantastically large glasses and sipped white wine every few seconds. At another dinner, I had used my bread to sop up what was left of the Caesar dressing from the salad on my plate. I wiped the plate clean and looked up to realize I'd made an unconscious and terrible mistake.

"Did you need more salad, dear?" asked Mr. Martin, peering at my plate over his glasses.

"Um, no thanks. I'm fine."

I put the last scrap of bread beside my plate, and then for no reason, or maybe because everyone was looking at me, I stuffed it in my mouth.

Things like that still happened around my in-laws, and so I didn't like to feel at a disadvantage—ever.

When John came home, I asked him almost immediately what he'd told his parents.

"Does that tea have caffeine?" he asked suspiciously, hanging his coat on the hook behind the door and inspecting the little tag that dangled from my mug. "Oh, chamomile. That's good."

"Yes, darling," I said. "I read the books, too."

He smiled and tugged gently on a strand of my hair, his signal for "I refuse to fight with you."

I repeated my question. "What did you say to your mom about my job?"

He sat down at our small kitchen table and started spreading peanut butter and jelly on a slice of pita bread. It was the marriage of Arab and American food—like hummus on a hoagie.

"My parents were just thinking that, you know, since we're having a baby soon . . . wouldn't it be better to quit the clothes shop so you can start sooner on your degree?"

"What degree, John? This is the part that baffles me—when did I ever say I was going back to school?"

He tilted his head to the side as he replied, "You did—and I remember this—you *did* say you were thinking of doing a business degree."

"*Thinking* is a key word here."

"And I want to support your decision—to be the kind of husband who encourages that."

"But I'm not ready to quit my job yet, John," I said firmly, using the quiet tone Baba had rarely had to use with me when I did something so wrong that Mama couldn't handle it. "I really like working at the clothes store—and I'm good at it. It's not rocket science, but it works for me."

"I know, but—and my mom made this point—you were once accepted to Penn, for Christ's sake. Your SAT scores were only slightly lower than mine, and I was forced into all those prep courses while you took it *cold*."

"And?" I couldn't imagine he'd actually had this conversation with his mother.

"There's a lot of *potential*, Hanan. That's all."

The dinner at his colleague's had been postponed for another week, but I didn't mention his mother's dinner invitation. Instead, I stayed up late in the basement, weaving gold strips through the bottom and sides of a dark brown basket.

Nadia lived in the old neighborhood with her mother. She kept her mom company—they held on to each other like entwined tree branches, twisting and, eventually, sharing one another's cloud of leaves. Their cloud of leaves was the sadness that had sprouted when Nadia's father was killed in a car accident.

I tried parking my car—an SUV, which John had insisted on buying for our upcoming family—in front of the apartment, but SUVs were not made for the city. I eventually parked it tightly between a Cabriolet and a Fiat on 10th Street, except I didn't know how I'd get it out again without ramming the Cabriolet's black rubber bumper and the Fiat's fender several times. But that was an obstacle I needn't worry about for at least another hour, I thought, as I stared up at the building. A blue stone hung inside the large bay window, placed there by my aunt to ward off the Evil Eye. Auntie Siham was a fanatic for blue stones, everyone knew, and they appeared in every room of her house, making me feel like I was being followed. Nadia never seemed to care, but I guess she just got used to it. When Uncle Nader died, the stones went up more fiercely than ever before. Above the stove, in the bedroom closet, dangling from the shower head, from the rearview mirror of their car. Mama had never agreed with me that Auntie Siham's obsession was weird. "Hanan, you don't understand *loss*," she said once in Arabic, standing in the living room, folding the pile of clean, fragrant laundry on the sofa. "Siham has lost more than you ever will in your whole life."

Nadia answered the door right away. She hugged me tightly. "That was pretty fast," I said, standing back on the front step to look at her.

She pointed upwards, and my eyes followed until I glimpsed the open second-floor window and the tiny white corner of a pillow peeking out over the sill. Of course. We sat up there a few minutes later, sipping Diet Cokes, our elbows entrenched in the pillows, looking down at 10th Street below us.

"I remember doing this when we were kids."

"We've come far, huh?" she said, laughing. Nadia's face was long and smooth, her long, aquiline nose delicate and aristocratic, sloping down to her full lips. When she smiled, her mouth almost met the corners of her eyes and her teeth became a half moon, sparkling and bright. She never wore makeup, though Aliyah, Reema, and I often tried to get her to put some lilac shadow on her lids, some brick red gloss on her lips, some mauve blush on her cheeks. But she resisted, saying she had no time to worry about makeup. She had the same philosophy about her hair—a silken, glossy black mass that she, unfortunately, kept tied up in a bun.

"Where's your mother?"

"Visiting yours."

I turned to her sharply, but she avoided my look, and continued gazing down at the boys playing Wiffle ball on the sidewalk below.

"I haven't seen my mom since a week before the wedding—it's been almost five months."

"Avoiding her?" she asked gently.

"Don't start with me," I replied, keeping my voice light.

"She misses you."

I pushed myself off the windowsill and stood before Nadia, my hands shaking. "Then she shouldn't have pushed me away."

"Haven't you *ever* been irrational, Hanan? So angry that you don't think about what you're saying?"

"No, but I'm getting there now." I couldn't keep the sarcastic edge from slipping into my voice.

"Come on." She moved over toward me, squinting tightly, like she was facing a bright light. "I know you have been that angry, so don't even play like you haven't. I've seen you go off on people like a firecracker."

"She really hurt me, Nadia."

"I know. But you know who's suffering most in all this? Your dad."

"God*damn*it." I walked out of the room, and into her kitchen, where I dumped out the soda and poured myself water. She followed me in and sat down at her kitchen table quietly. She knew the impact her words had on me. She had played the kryptonite card: Baba. He was my weak spot, and would always be. I had not seen him since the wedding either, and I doubted I would ever see him unless Mama was at his side.

Nadia looked like she expected an answer, but I didn't give her one. Later, we went back to the window, where we listened to a homeless man, with graying hair floating below his shoulders, mutter furiously to himself as he slouched toward Pierce Street. Nadia called to the boys playing Wiffle ball not to tease him, and they obeyed, waiting quietly until he passed.

I left an hour later, bumping the Fiat's fender twice before I emerged from the tight parking space. As I roared up 10th Street, I saw Auntie Siham walking toward her house. She wore a long, black trench coat and her hair was pulled back in a black headwrap. Though she dressed simply, Auntie Siham had always had a fashion penchant that my own mother lacked—she looked like she spent more than ten minutes picking out her clothes and fixing her hair. She rarely wore makeup, but she didn't need it. At home, she wore baggy housedresses, but her nails were elegantly manicured. Even her walk was stylish—her feet graced the sidewalk in long, even strides, darting over an occasional puddle or sidestepping gracefully around a half-eaten hot dog that might appear suddenly on a South Philly street.

Nadia would be waiting at the window, and call down a greeting when she saw her mother turn the corner. "I'll make some *majad-darah* for dinner," Auntie would yell up, "something easy," and they would talk about their days in the kitchen while the rice and lentils boiled and the onions simmered in yellow oil. After dinner, they'd curl up on the couch with two plates of Auntie's *kanafa*, taking small bites of the cheese pastry while laughing over an Egyptian comedy on the Arabic satellite TV. Maybe later in the evening, Nadia would work on her laptop while Auntie sat beside her, crocheting a blanket or embroidering a pillow or peeling apples for a cake she planned to bake the next morning.

Auntie Siham looked up at my car as I passed her. I waved. She blew me a kiss in return.

As I drove up Roosevelt Boulevard, I thought about the weeks before the wedding, when Auntie Siham had pleaded with Mama to give up fighting with me. I went to Nadia's house one afternoon, having just returned from the bridal boutique. They'd tailored a dress with a high waist, from which large lengths of tulle cascaded down— all to cover my slightly bloated belly. I had the shopgirls snap some Polaroids of me, and these were what I brought to show Nadia.

"Do I look like a cow?"

"No way!" she replied, scrutinizing the photos. "You're only eight weeks, for Christ's sake. Why would you think you look fat?"

"Well, I feel like a boat." I rubbed my belly. "Like a cruise liner, actually." Although most people claimed they couldn't tell I was pregnant, I could see their curious glances at my belly, as well as at my breasts, which had swelled to twice their normal size since the little pregnancy test stick had turned blue.

John liked to rub my ankles, which felt and looked as broad as tree trunks, massaging them to help me relax. Even though I was still living with Aliyah, he came over all the time, bringing a movie and a healthy take-out meal that usually involved salad and tofu. "We both need to eat healthy, not just you," he explained.

But sitting on Nadia's couch in her cozy living room, I couldn't imagine having more children, at least not for a while. The fact that in less than three weeks I would marry John and move into a house in University City—this still shocked me. Everything—marriage, children, a house—all of it was happening at once, and I sometimes realized that I couldn't quite catch my breath.

The doorbell rang, and Nadia jumped to answer it. Auntie Siham murmured her thanks and eased through the doorway sideways, carrying a large package wrapped in brown paper.

I rose and tried to take the box from her, but she and Nadia wouldn't let me touch it. "You shouldn't be carrying or lifting anything heavy," Auntie Siham chided, stretching out her neck so I could plant a kiss on one cheek and then on the other.

"What is that, Mama?" Nadia asked, taking it and placing it on the dining room table. "Is this the card that came in the mail yesterday?"

"Yes, I had to go pick it up at the post office—I went there," she said, sitting down and looking at me with a small smile, "right after I visited your mother."

I leaned back on the couch and crossed my legs at the ankle. "I'm glad to hear that—at least she's still talking to everyone, even if I'm not one of the lucky chosen few."

"Actually, I went there with Huda, because Reema talked her into going."

"Not Auntie Lamis?"

"Well, Aliyah's mother has a different opinion," Auntie Siham said tactfully, snapping her fingers at Nadia, who got up and poured lemonade into three tall glasses.

"I guess I've turned out the way Auntie Lamis always thought I would," I said with a sigh. "So how is my mother doing?" I asked Auntie Siham. "I hope she's not driving my father crazy."

"Your father looks a little pale these days," she replied, taking a dainty sip from her lemonade and leaving a pale pink imprint of her lips on the glass's rim. My mother never wore lipstick, or makeup at all. "He seems worn down. Tired."

"You would be too, Auntie, if you had to listen to my mother all day." I paused before asking my next question, because I was sure the answer would disappoint me. "Did she ask about me?"

She shook her head, a small, tight motion, twice to the left.

"But why don't you open the box?" she said, standing up. "What's in it will put a smile on your face." She carried it over to me, and Nadia moved the lemonade tray off the coffee table so I could rest the box upon it.

Once I sliced through the sealing tape with my key, the lids flapped down to the side and I could see that the box was stuffed with tissue paper. I reached my hands in, pulling out wispy, transparent sheets until my eye fell upon a crown of pearls, resting snugly in the center of the box. I tugged on it gently, releasing it from its cardboard cage, and to my delight, I saw—as I lifted it out—that a long, scalloped white lace veil was attached to it.

"They don't know how to make wedding veils here in America," Auntie Siham said. "So I ordered one for you from Jerusalem, from the same woman who made mine."

Speechless, I was shocked to realize that my throat, suddenly dry, was clenching wildly, and that tears were gathering behind my eyes, ready to march down upon my cheeks.

"Don't tell us you don't like it!"

"It's gorgeous," Nadia said, snatching it up and placing it on my head. "Of course she likes it." She pulled me to my feet, drawing me before the hallway mirror.

"I love it," I exclaimed, gazing at my reflection in the mirror: my flushed cheeks, watery eyes, and the cascade of delicate white lace falling from my shoulders, the rows of carefully sewn pearl beads that framed my face.

For the first time since I'd started planning this wedding, I felt like a bride. Auntie Siham had made me so.

I had often envisioned the camps where Mama grew up. After all, I'd spent almost all my life hearing about them, so it was natural to picture them for myself: cement shacks with hastily thatched roofs, children running barefoot on dirt paths, sidestepping donkey dung as they scampered about, old men sitting on wooden crates playing *tarneeb* with a badly worn deck of cards. The women in the camp wore clean but threadbare clothes, and flashed smiles that displayed missing teeth. At times I felt my imagination fail me, so I would ask Mama for the details, for the nuggets of information that would help correct the picture in my mind.

Was there food?

Not much.

Was there water?

Barely.

Were there schools?

Not really.

What was there?

Only the hope of a better life.

Only my family.

Only love.

How did you leave?

Your grandparents struggled to get working permits or even visas, but it didn't work. They snuck us all in through Canada instead, so when I met your father and we married, I became a citizen through him.

What about grandfather? And my aunts and uncles?

Your Uncle Ibrahim got a green card too, because he married. Your grandfather had to go back home. He died there, in that filthy camp.

Whenever she talked about Sidi, whom I'd never met, she got angry. Her head would bend down again to scrub at the pot or pan I'd interrupted her from cleaning. Her brows would collide in an angry line.

Are you mad at me?

Jesus, Mary, and Joseph, *ya binit!* You ask too many questions.

The dinner at John's colleague's house was scheduled for the following Saturday night. I tried on six different outfits before finally settling on black trousers and a frilly, pink maternity blouse that Aliyah had bought for me. I felt very underdressed, even though John told me I looked great—but he said that before we were married, when I was single, pre-commitment, and pre-pregnant. I felt even worse when we arrived at the party, where I stood out like a bright, pink pimple in a room where everyone wore black: black pantsuits, blazers, cardigans, trousers—and turtlenecks. Oh, the turtlenecks, tucked into the waistbands of black trousers, cinched with slim, black leather belts.

"I don't want to stay long," I warned John, but he squeezed my hand as a warning because our hostess was arriving. John had briefed me about her in the car: the chair of the sociology department, she had earned her PhD in the '70s, spent ten years studying gender issues in the Mideast and South Asia, and she was one of the people supporting John's bid for a tenure-track position.

"If I can just publish an article based on the book I'm researching," he explained, "I'll be in."

I hadn't asked him what his book was about, because he'd explained it to me before, and I knew it related to adolescents and peer pressure and his dissertation committee had thought it brilliant. I had, however, perfected a slight smile and arch of the right eyebrow that implied, "Wow, darling. That is amazing. I'm fascinated by your intelligence and insight."

I slipped that expression on at the party, as John began explaining to me that the chair of the department was working on a new book.

"About what, may I ask?" I was becoming a pro, I mused, with an alarming aptitude for feigning interest.

"Actually, you might be particularly interested," she said, leading us through clusters of professors in wool blazers (black, of course) and into the dining room, where the long, oval-shaped table was set up as a mini-bar. "Wine?"

John took a glass of merlot, while I pointed apologetically at my swollen belly, giggling along with her when she got my point (not too swiftly, despite her degree).

"So the book is about the ways in which Arab women—especially Muslim women—learn about or enter into politics in the Middle East." She tilted her chin upwards, delighted with herself. "It's based primarily on my own observations, though it relies somewhat on scholarship. I wanted to take a break from academic writing and write something that was almost a memoir."

"Great idea," John commented. "Jules Kravinsky just did something similar about his time, his field work in . . ."

"Yes . . . in China. I am reading that now." She turned back to me. "I wonder if you might be interested in reading my first draft."

She and John both gazed at me intently. "Read it?" I finally said.

"Yes." She waited attentively, while John began to look anxious.

"For what?"

"Well, for *authenticity*. I want an Arab woman's perspective on how *real* my writing is, how genuine and *accurate* my observations."

"But, but I'm not Arab."

"Oh?" She looked at John, whose cheeks swam in dark red blotches. "I thought you said once that your wife is Palestinian— and," she added, returning to me, "Hanan is a distinctly Arabic name." She pronounced it perfectly, delivering the "h" from the back of her throat instead of the upper cavern of her mouth.

"My parents are both from Palestine. Or Israel. You know, the West Bank. Whatever they call it now." I paused for a deep breath. I had never been comfortable saying "Palestine," because I never knew what kind of reaction I'd get. Once I saw my mother tell someone in Safeway that she was from Palestine, and the woman looked at her like she was an alien and said, "There is no such country," before walking away. The pathetic, confused look on Mama's face burned itself into my memory, always igniting my anger when I thought of it. "But even my father was born here," I told our hostess. "Only my mother is actually an immigrant."

"And," I added with a tone of what I thought was finality, "I've never been to the Middle East in my entire life."

She walked away soon after that, excusing herself to attend to other guests. John suggested, in a strangled voice, that we "mingle for a bit."

We hung out at the cheese and crackers station. "Quite a feast, isn't it, John?" a colleague remarked casually in passing, and John nodded. "Absolutely! I'm already stuffed!" And I was thinking to my-self that my mother would die laughing if she heard the word "feast" used to describe a few tables set up with cheese, water crackers, and some bowls of fruit.

I smirked slightly, and John asked me what was so funny.

"Nothing."

"What? What is it?" His lips compressed tightly and his eyebrows furrowed.

"God, why are you so *tense*?" I asked him, getting annoyed. "What is wrong with you?"

"If you haven't noticed, we're at a department function with my colleagues—"

"No shit."

"Could you not talk like that please?"

"I've always talked like that."

"Well, not tonight, please."

"So *this* is your lovely wife," I heard, as two older men approached us, one with a shag of white curly hair and the other a short man, who was bursting out of his herringbone sportcoat.

"Dr. Farrington. Dr. Keriakis—both senior professors in our department," John said, and I dutifully shook hands. I caught John's eye, and he winked, his face suffused with red. He was nervous, and, to my own dismay, I felt my own nerves become suddenly jittery.

"How do you pronounce your name again, dear?" asked Keriakis.

"Hanan," I said, deliberately softening the hard, initial "H" as I'd done all my life for people who would only look at me quizzically if I did not.

"A Middle Eastern name, no?"

"Yes."

"Ah . . . thought so," said Farrington. "From which region do you hail?"

"From 10th and Tasker," I replied, laughing. But neither Farrington nor Keriakis cracked a smile. Farrington looked confused, and John looked like he would collapse.

"Beg your pardon?"

"10th and Tasker . . . I was making a joke. I grew up here in Philadelphia."

"Oh, yes! Of course! But where in the *Middle East* do you come from?" he repeated, as if I had not understood the question. "Lebanon, Egypt?"

"Palestine . . . My parents are from Jerusalem."

"Yes, yes," Keriakis said. "I've been to Israel several times."

I shrugged. "Well, my parents always referred to it as Palestine, so . . ."

"Of course, most naturally they would." And Farrington seemed to think Keriakis's remark funny, and they chuckled.

I couldn't help but think they were laughing at me—but I also couldn't understand why. I glanced at John for help, but he was not looking at me, just grinning at the two men.

"It was good to meet you, Hanan," Keriakis said. "We will say our good evenings now, since we are leaving."

"So soon?" John asked, shaking the hands proferred to him.

"We must. We're attending the conference in San Francisco this weekend, and our flight leaves at 7 in the a.m."

When Keriakis came to shake my hand, he held it for a few seconds. "It was especially good to meet you, Hanan. I hope we'll meet again soon. I'd like to hear more about Palestine—it's a cause dear to my heart. And I mean that," he added quietly.

He leaned in—why, I wasn't sure, but my instinct took over, and I kissed his cheek, which was right next to my mouth. I did it because that is how I kissed all my uncles and cousins and relatives . . . a handshake and a kiss on the cheek. But I knew, even as my lips had made a slight indent on his soft, weathered cheek, that I was making a big, big mistake.

He pulled back, laughing, his wrinkled face a shade darker. "That was a pleasant surprise. I was only going to tell you that I spent a lot of time studying in the Middle East—and now I feel right at home. I guess you can take a girl out of Palestine, but . . . well, you know the rest." Everyone else chuckled, but when I glanced at John, he deliberately looked away from me.

On the ride home, as he cruised along the Schuylkyll Expressway, the city skyline, the lights on Boathouse Row whizzing by us, he exploded.

"What were you *thinking?*" he roared, his hands gripping the steering wheel. "That whole evening was *mortifying*. Do you understand me? Mortifying."

"Well, why are you blaming me? I didn't want to go in the first place."

"I cannot believe you kissed him. A goddamned professor emeritus of the department."

"John—"

"And what was all that stuff—'I'm not an Arab.' What was that about?"

"I'm not an Arab. That woman—"

"—the chair of the department—"

"Whoever the fuck she was."

"Oh, right. Straight to the foul language . . ."

"John, that woman, she wanted me to be an expert on her new book. Do I look like a walking almanac on the Middle East?"

"You could have at least showed interest," he added, suddenly quiet.

"She caught me off guard."

"That's what . . ." he started, then stopped.

"What?"

"That's what an educated person would have done."

It was quiet, and then I said, sharply, "Fuck you, John."

> Hanan,
>
> I don't know if you'll ever speak to me again. I probably don't deserve it. I'm sorry for what I said the other night. But the truth is that what I said is actually how I feel. And even more, I now question how wise it was for us to get married in the first place. Something has changed—I don't know what, and I wish I did know so I could try to fix it—and I can't continue like this. We're not happy. Don't you feel that?
>
> I'm going to my parents to stay there for a while. I think you probably don't want to see me anyway, and

I don't want to add to your stress. I will find an apart-
ment of my own later. The house is yours. I'll keep
making payments.

My pager is on, cell phone on, all day and night.
I will check on you every day.

We disappointed each other, but I promise not to
disappoint our baby. I'm sorry if anything I wrote here
has hurt you.

John

Michael came five months after John left. I was in the basement, soaking long flat pieces of wood in dye when my water broke, pooling onto the seat of the hardwood chair. I called Reema, who had spent the last two nights at my house. She raced down the steps, the heavy lug bottoms of her Doc Martens pounding on the wooden staircase.

"It's time?"

"Yes!" For a second, I forgot all about John, caught up in the elation that soon I would be a mother. "I can't wait to see you," I whispered fiercely, wrapping my arms around my belly. Even though I could feel my joints loosening, my uterus thumping wildly, and the fact that I was sitting in a puddle of my own amniotic fluid—I never felt so in control in my life. I was powerful, collected, in charge of not only my own life but that of my baby.

I chose the name Michael. An Americanized version of my father's name, Michel.

As I lay there, with Michael in my arms, I looked into his enormous eyes, fingered his thick mop of black hair, and fell into a deep trance, a sense of love that filled my throat and threatened to spill out of my eyes. The intense loneliness that had seized me as I read John's note months earlier, as I scurried through the house, noting his half-emptied closet, his clothes picked out of the dryer—confirming that *yes,* yes, he'd actually done it and left me—that loneliness washed away now as I gazed in wonder at my son.

The only love I'd ever experienced that even came close to this moment was with my father, when he would hug me or kiss my cheek and then pat that spot, as if to ensure it would adhere. That was the memory that flooded immediately into my mind. And so I named my son Michael after my father, after Baba.

Reema crept into my room, her face beaming. "*Salamat*, Imm Michael."

"You heard?"

"The nurse told me." She sat gingerly on the edge of my bed, peering down at Michael. "Your dad will be thrilled."

"I know. I was actually thinking that naming him after Baba sticks to our tradition, anyway, doesn't it?"

"Most men name their first sons after their fathers," Reema said, nodding. "That's why my brother is named Ahmad."

"And why Aliyah's brother Nabeel has his name," I added. "So I'm just following tradition, since my father doesn't have a son."

The door opened again, and in walked Nadia and Aliyah, crying and laughing at once.

"Hanan! *Habibti!* Let me see him."

"*Habibti! Albi!* I can't believe you're a mommy. What's his name?"

"Michael."

"Ohh . . ." They both got teary-eyed and quiet, and then the four of us began sniffling as they crowded around the bed and took turns holding him.

"*Sm'allah al'ei*, Hanan! Your son is a bull!"

"Look at all this hair! He already needs a haircut."

"Wait until you see the outfit Auntie Reema bought for you, *habibi*. You're going to look so handsome!"

The door creaked open again, and it was George. "I just looked on the patient list and saw your name, Hanan," he said, walking in timidly, one hand holding a chart and the other fingering the collar of his white lab coat. "*Mabrouk.*"

"Thanks, George. Do you want to see him?"

George put his chart down and came closer, avoiding meeting Nadia's eyes. She, in turn, picked up her purse and said she would go home and get her mother, who wanted to see the baby. She left abruptly, but George did not flinch—he gazed intently at Michael, offering him a finger. Michael grabbed it firmly and George chuckled, "Your son is strong as a bull!"

I almost told him, "That's what Nadia said," but thought better of it and kept quiet.

"I'll stop in later," he promised, and impulsively kissed my cheek. "God bless him."

As soon as he left, I muttered, "That was awkward."

"I still can't believe they haven't worked it out," Reema said.

Aliyah nodded. "Me too."

"She's been feeling lousy—depressed—since the accident," I added. They both nodded vigorously. "Something has to change."

I remember that night clearly, more than a year ago, when we'd headed to the Poconos in George's car. George had been in a great mood, and he'd turned around to say something to John and me in the backseat, slipping unknowingly past the stop sign, in front of a car barreling in from the right. Nadia had been the most badly hurt—the car had hit us on her side—while the rest of us walked away with bad scratches and blackened bruises. She had slipped into a coma for days before coming back to us. Both her legs and her hip had been broken, and she'd spent months recovering.

"Poor Nadia," murmured Reema. "Remember how much time we all spent trying to cheer her up—us, George, John?"

"John!" I exclaimed, startling my friends. "I guess I have to tell him he is a new father." In the excitement of meeting my son, I'd forgotten about my husband.

John arrived around noon. He'd come the night before as well, but I'd been too exhausted to recall anything. He carried a small box of chocolates and a large coffee cup.

"How's the new mom doing?" he asked, his eyes on Michael sleeping in his bassinet.

"Fine," I replied. "I just finished feeding him. He's doing pretty well, the nurse said. They weigh them every day."

He put the chocolate and coffee on the small, rolling tray beside my bed. "These are for you—some things you couldn't have while you were pregnant."

"I still can't have caffeine if I'm breastfeeding," I said testily.

"It's decaf," he shot back.

"Oh. OK." I sipped the hot liquid slowly. It had been a really long time since I'd enjoyed good coffee, as I'd been too paranoid to even drink decaf during the past nine months.

"Can I pick him up?" John asked timidly. "I'm afraid to wake him up."

I gazed over at John, standing hesitantly by the bassinet. His glasses had slipped down his nose till they hovered at the very edge, and his light scarf dangled unevenly around his neck. Suddenly, I felt a surge of affection for him, and the intensity of it shocked me. I forced myself to remember that this was the same man who'd left me while I was pregnant and that he deserved only my scorn.

"He won't wake up. He sleeps like a rock," I said matter-of-factly, enjoying a feeling of superiority, of knowing more than he did already about our infant son. The feeling only lasted fleetingly, however, and I was soon submerged in an unfamiliar emotional current as I watched John hold Michael, carefully cradling Michael's head in his left elbow. Sadness, perhaps, that we were not a single unit, that I'd testily responded "He's not in the picture" when the girl at the registration desk asked me about the baby's father at check-in. Other fathers in the rooms down the hall had spent the night. I couldn't help but feel that I'd been cheated.

Michael and I went home the next day. Aliyah picked us up and took care of getting the car seat installed in my car. When we pulled up to the house, I saw the mailbox wrapped in blue streamers and a dozen blue balloons flapping in the breeze.

"Aliyah! Did you do this for me?"

"Nope. We did it for Michael."

I carried him carefully out of the car and walked slowly up the steps, still sore, while Aliyah carried my suitcase. The front door was flung open by Reema, yelling "Welcome home!"

Inside, Reema, Nadia, and Auntie Siham had prepared a lunch for us—a tray of grape leaves, chicken with sumac, and *fattoush* salad. They had draped more blue streamers around the living room, making the scene festive. I put Michael's car seat down and burst into tears, stunned by my own reaction.

"It's just my hormones," I mumbled unconvincingly as my friends surrounded me, hugging me and wiping their own tears. "Really, I'm OK. I'll be fine."

My days after Michael's birth flowed together, lapping gently against the shore of my mind. Aliyah, Reema, and Nadia had pooled their money and purchased a light blue jogging stroller for me, which I used almost every day.

It was April, and University City came alive. I usually walked during the morning hours, around 10 A.M., and I met other young mothers doing the same. People jogged or strolled past and smiled at us. I often received a "How handsome he is" or "Isn't he precious?" and I couldn't help beaming. I also realized that in all my months of pregnancy, I hadn't explored my own neighborhood even once.

On Walnut Street, I noticed a gift shop, "Cabbages and Kings," with an inviting window display. The panes of the window were painted in a springtime scene, and various dolls were arranged like children playing among the flowers. I left Michael's stroller inside the entrance and hoisted him into the sling that I had draped across my torso. I opened the brightly painted purple door, which prompted a bell to tinkle, and entered. Michael screeched, but I patted his bottom gently and pulled him closer to my heart, humming a little Arabic ditty Mama used to croon to me. I only knew the rhythm, not the words—but Michael was satisfied nonetheless.

"Hi there," came a gentle voice from behind the counter. "Who's this good-looking young man come to visit us?" The woman had a mass of red hair streaked with gray, tied up in a bun atop her head, and a delicate pair of gold-rimmed glasses were perched on her wide, squat nose.

"His name is Michael," I said, approaching and holding him up to her, as if for inspection. "I'm Hanan."

"He's a perfect angel," she said, smiling. "My name is Anne, I own this shop and most of these are my creations. Let me know if you need any help or have any questions."

"Your own creations?" I repeated. "Did you design that display window?"

"Oh yes. And I made everything in it—those dolls and the soap baskets. And the candles too."

"Amazing. What a talent." I gazed around the store, soaking it in. The etched glass and beaded wind chimes that hung from the ceiling, the baskets of candles that were attractively arranged and decorated, the small, painted boxes, decorated with flowers and rosettes.

"You know, I also have a bit of a creative streak," I said, turning back to Anne, who had resumed what she'd been working on before I entered—painting a pink rose onto the wooden surface of a drink coaster.

"What kinds of crafts do you enjoy?"

"I make hand-woven baskets. It's a Middle Eastern design, with colored flat straws."

"What part of the Middle East?" she asked, leaning forward on the counter, planting her elbows on the glass.

"Pal- The Palestinian territories." I responded.

"Interesting." Anne had stopped painting, and was looking at me thoughtfully. "You should show me some of your work."

"Maybe I will." Before I left, spurred on by Michael's relentless gnawing on my covered nipple, his gums hurting me even through the layers of clothing, I bought a small yellow candle labelled "Chamomile/Honey Candle. For relaxation and soothing relief from stress." I paid my $6.95 and said goodbye to Anne, put Michael in his stroller, and ushered him home.

I fed him, watching as he sucked eagerly, frantically, emptying both breasts. "Poor little guy. I didn't know you'd get so hungry already." Michael's feeding and sleeping schedule were a mystery to me—I relied on books and Internet sites to tell me what to do with my child.

When he'd fallen asleep, his lips still wrapped around my nipple, I gingerly detached and laid him down gently into the bassinet. I lit the candle and placed it on the coffee table, watching its flame and breathing in the gentle scent.

As soon as my mind turned to John, I went downstairs to the basement and brought up the new basket I was working on. I'd promised myself that whenever John crept into my thoughts, I would not waste the time in a daze over him—which would have been quite simple to do. At least I would be productive—wash dishes, empty the diaper pail, fold clean laundry.

Now I was occupied by the memory of this morning, when John had come to pick up a few more items. I had let him in and told him not to be loud because Michael was asleep.

"Wow, does this boy just eat and sleep all day long?" he asked, putting on a false smile and a high pitch in his voice.

I shrugged and walked into the kitchen, where I was reorganizing the pantry. He followed me in and leaned against the counter, watching me toss out expired boxes of Raisin Bran, strawberry PopTarts, and Oreo cookies—all the things that were his particular favorites.

John chose his battles wisely, and he did so this time as well. "You know," he began, ignoring the unopened package that sailed into the trash can, "I'm staying at my parents' house now. We should talk about what happens to this house."

"You can have it. Michael and I are moving in with Aliyah eventually, as soon as she gets a bigger apartment. Should be about another month or two. You could put this place on the market now." *Pfomp!* A box of Grapenuts landed in the can.

John swallowed audibly. "Why don't you just live here, Hanan? Aliyah can move in with you. What does she pay for rent? $900 a month?"

"About."

"Tell her to pay $600, and I'll put in the other $600 for the mortgage. And I'll give you extra money for Michael too, since you probably won't be able to work."

I ignored his assumption, though I bristled at the suggestion that I could not work. I also wanted to be able to say to him, "Keep your money," but I could not financially do that. Suddenly I felt miserable about the fact that I really did need him.

"Hanan," he continued, "I was just offered the job. An assistant professor's position at Drexel University."

I turned to face him. He was smiling. It took me a few seconds, but I finally said, "Congratulations."

"The salary is pretty good, enough to get me a small apartment near campus, plus help me pay the mortgage here. Plus an allowance for you and Michael."

"Please *don't* call it an allowance."

He paused, then said, "OK, sorry. You're right."

"I'm glad all your dreams have come true and everything, but mine haven't exactly worked out."

"I just want to be part of Michael's life, Hanan. He is mine too."

"I am not going to *keep* you away from your son, John. I'm a better person than you give me credit for."

"I never meant it that way—"

"Of course you did," I interrupted him, struggling to keep my voice down. "You clearly told me once, while I was still pregnant, that because I cannot reconcile with my own mother I would make a pretty lousy mother. Don't you remember that?"

"Hanan—"

"So guess what, John? I didn't grow up in a perfect family like you. My mom was a tyrant and I know she loved me but she never understood me. She refused to come to the wedding, for God's sake, when she found out I wasn't a fucking *virgin*. OK?"

"OK."

"So would you please stop treating me like a failure?"

"OK." He sounded conciliatory, but I knew he just wanted to leave. And I wanted him to leave too, so I could sit down and cry without an audience.

The sun blazed in the sky, unprotected by even a wisp of a cloud. I could have cursed myself for forgetting to pack my sunblock. The thin skin at the bridge of my nose was already starting to tingle and stretch. By tonight I would have a ridiculous tan line across my face, but I didn't want to remove my sunglasses. It was just too bright—too hot. Thank God I'd left Michael at home with Aliyah.

"I have to do what to your breasts?" she'd asked me this morning, as I packed my car with boxes of junk I hoped would sell at the community flea market. I had also taken along some of my basket designs, since the sale was advertised as a craft show as well as a flea market.

"Not to my breasts—to my breast milk." Aliyah, though I adored her, had an annoying habit of listening to only part of what I said rather than hearing out the whole thing. "You just have to heat it in a pan, with some water. I put the pan out for you, and the milk is in the plastic bags in the freezer."

"I'll just zap it in the microwave," she said sleepily, picking up Michael from his crib. He stirred restlessly.

"No, don't do that. It's not safe. Some study I read about showed that it releases toxins or something. Just use the pan. Are you OK?"

She looked bewildered, standing in her red terry bathrobe, with mismatched socks, rocking Michael in her arms.

"*Habibti*, I pump my breasts during the day when Michael isn't feeding—so they don't stay so full. That's what that little machine is in the bedroom—my pump."

"Why don't you just give him formula?"

"It's too expensive," I said, grunting as I lifted a box of John's books off the floor. "Anyway, our moms breastfed us until we were practically walking up to them and asking for it."

"That's true," she agreed, almost reluctantly. "It's just funny to think that we're turning into our moms."

"I'm trying not to do that," I'd joked, then paused when I saw her expression—a rolling of the eyes and a slight shake of the head. "What?"

"You're too hard on your mom—it's like everyone loves her, except you."

"That's fine," I returned quickly, "because she likes everyone except me."

Before she could say anything else, I'd kissed the slumbering Michael's forehead and winked at Aliyah before struggling out the front door with my burden.

At the community craft sale and flea market, I set up most of my items on a small card table and laid out the rest in boxes on the ground. The sale was being held along Locust Walk, which cut through the University of Pennsylvania campus. It seemed as if the whole neighborhood had come out and set up stalls to sell their chipped coffee mugs, five-hundred-piece puzzles, mismatched Lenox china, Ann Taylor tweed blazers, and worn Coach leather handbags.

One elderly man strolled by my table, carrying a golf club bag over his shoulders. Rich, probably a doctor, I thought. He grinned at me and peered at my sale items politely.

"How's business, pretty lady?"

"Not bad, I guess—I only set up an hour ago."

"You've been here since seven?"

"That's when they told us to set up."

"I see, I see." He picked up one of John's books—*A People's History of the United States*—and leafed through it. John's mother had given it to him for Christmas last year. I realized suddenly that many of my items for sale had been given to us by John's mother—there was the chenille sweater she's given me for my birthday, one that had a wide collar and tunic shaping, the kind of thing I would never wear. I looked at it more closely—it still had a Macy's sales tag, with the price ripped off, dangling from the sleeve. I also spied some of the baby outfits she had bought for Michael; he was growing so fast that hardly anything fit him any longer. I made a mental note to shop at the other tables myself to see if anyone was selling used baby clothes cheaply.

"My daughter would like this book . . . how much do you want for it?"

"Two?"

"I like that price. You have yourself a deal, pretty lady."

He pulled his wallet out of his back pocket, but paused and then knelt down to look at my baskets, the top edge of his golf bag tapping my table. I'd brought three of them with me: one had green and black weaves; one had a red, white, and blue pattern; and one was plain straw-colored, with some dark brown edging.

"How much for these?"

"Thirty dollars," I said, trying to keep my voice casual. He didn't react, just nodded. "They're handmade, by yours truly."

"Is that right?"

"It's my hobby."

He stood up. "They're beautiful—you have a good eye for design." I really thought he would buy one, but then he just pulled two dollar bills out of his wallet and handed them to me.

"Thanks," I replied, forcing a smile.

"Good luck."

"Have a good one."

For the next hour, I stayed busy. People came by and bought my old sweaters, CDs, and most of John's books. One pregnant woman bought all of my maternity clothes and all of Michael's newborn baby outfits. I charged her $25 for everything, and she was thrilled.

"Baby clothes are so expensive," she said, handing me the money. "I just hope you're having a boy!"

She laughed, her brass beaded earrings tinkling as her head shook. "Even if I'm not, she wouldn't know the difference."

"It's not healthy for a girl to be dressed exclusively in pink, anyway," said a young woman wearing horn-rimmed glasses, who was fingering one of my sweaters.

"I agree," said the mother-to-be. "Kids shouldn't be put into categories."

"Especially not from birth," I chimed in.

The mother-to-be moved along, after wishing us a good day. A young man, tall with ruddy skin and blue eyes, met up with her and draped his arm around her shoulders. I suddenly felt a twist of jealousy, and self-pity threatened to sweep over me.

"Miss? How much are these baskets?"

The person speaking to me had a gentle voice, articulate, enunciating her letters exactly.

"Thirty," I replied, looking more closely at her. She had snowy hair and soft, liquidy brown eyes, but her cheeks were smooth, soft.

"That's what my husband said, I think," she said, nodding as if we'd just agreed on something of significance. "He sent me over here to look at them."

"The man with the golf clubs?"

She grinned, her eyes crinkling at the corners. "That's my Bob." She picked up the straw-colored basket with the dark-brown edging and examined it carefully. "He said one of them would match the colors of my kitchen, so it must be this one. I just got new cabinets and new butcher-block counters in exactly this color. This would work well as a fruit basket for the main counter."

"It is pretty," said the young woman with the glasses, who knelt herself to look at my baskets.

Within five minutes, I had made sixty dollars. I called Aliyah at the house—"Pack up Michael and bring me all the baskets on my table in the basement—quick, quick!"

"Breast milk and baskets," she muttered. "You need a freaking secretary."

In June, Michael turned three months old, and I drove him to South Philadelphia to meet his grandparents.

I had finally broken down—the day before Father's Day—and called my parents' house. I actually had to look up the phone number in my cell phone log since I had not dialed it in over a year. Baba answered, thankfully, and I was so relieved to hear his voice that I realized I must have been afraid I'd have to speak to my mother.

"Yes, *please* come," Baba said. "I cannot wait to see my grandson."

"His name is . . . it's Michael."

"I know," he said quietly. "I heard. Thank you."

When I pulled up in front of my parents' house, I noticed Joey and Sammy, the neighbor's two young sons, lounging on their stoop, exchanging bubble gum pack cards. When they saw me, they shouted at me to stop and scurried to move two folding chairs that were marking a parking space in front of my parents' house. "Your dad told us to save the spot," Joey shouted, as I backed my SUV and slid in.

"Jeez—that's a huge truck!" Sammy exclaimed. "Did your guy give it to you when he dumped you?" He was stunned into silence when his older brother promptly whacked his arm.

"That's OK, Sammy. Wanna meet my boy?" I got out and opened the back door, unbuckling a sleepy Michael out of his seat.

"Man, he's so little!" Joey said, standing on his toes to see the baby.

"He looks fake," Sammy declared.

"How come you get to meet my grandson before I do?" Baba stood behind the screen door, grinning widely as he watched us. I had to restrain a look of dismay. Baba was shriveled and frail, his once erect posture now slumped, as if his spine had melted away.

"Hi Baba," I said in the cheeriest voice I could muster. "I'll come in so you can meet him." I kissed both Joey and Sammy on their foreheads. "Thanks for saving my spot. Say hi to your mom for me."

Baba held the door wide, and I handed in the carrying seat to him, then stepped inside with Michael in my arms. I kissed Baba's cheeks, twice on each side, and then turned to see Mama standing by the coffee table, her hands folded in front of her. Her hair was shorter, curled, neatly trimmed and soft around her ears. She wore the same clothes I'd always seen her wear—long black pants and a baggy, button-down shirt, sprayed with tropical flowers and prints. On her feet were her signature black house slippers with the wooden soles.

"*Ahlan wa sahlan*, Hanan," she said, a hesitant look on her face. She made no move to approach me, so neither did I. I instinctively knew—I knew she had interpreted my visit as a signal of defeat on my part, my way of saying, "You were so right, Mama. That damned *Amerkani*—he knocked me up and then he left me. I should have listened to you." Determined not to let her feel satisfied or victorious, I focused my attention on the person I had really come to see—Baba.

"This is Michael," I said, "and he's really excited to meet you." I tried to put my sleepy son in Baba's arms, but Baba insisted on sitting down first. As he sank down into the cushions of the large, green fabric sofa, I gently laid Michael in his lap. Baba's left arm instinctively slid up under Michael's neck, supporting his bobbing head.

Michael slowly awoke, arriving out of his groggy fog to see a stranger peering down at him. And so he screeched and screeched, crying until his face was suffused with color—"just like his father," I thought, and took him back to soothe him. Rather than look hurt, Baba chuckled. "Layla," he said to my mother, "do you hear the voice on this boy?"

Mama, I realized, had moved up behind me, gazing down at Michael. "Shhhh . . ." she whispered softly to him, and Michael, who obviously intended on displeasing me today, ceased his screeching and gazed in wonderment at my mother.

"*Shater, habibi* . . ." she cooed. "*Bit hib Teta*, Mi-keel?" She clucked her tongue at him, and my son actually gurgled in delight. His first quasi-laugh.

"How about some lemonade?" Baba asked, breaking the brief silence. "Layla, get us three glasses, please? It's so humid today, and summer only just got started."

"It's been hot alright," I agreed, while Mama bustled off to the kitchen, her wooden sandals clacking sharply on the wooden floor of the dining room, then issuing a higher, sharper sound when her heels hit the tiles of the kitchen floor. "I'm glad you guys finally have an air conditioner down here," I added, nodding at the unit in the front window.

"Had to. It was getting to be too much. And upstairs was worse—it was like murder trying to sleep last summer."

"I can imagine," I said, turning Michael so he could face my father. "How are you feeling?"

"OK." He tickled Michael gently, tapping the tip of his nose.

"Come on, Mikey," I silently begged my son. "Laugh for your grandfather." But he didn't—he just stared at Baba confusedly, and Baba at last surrendered by kissing his cheek and then patting the spot with his fingers.

"Just OK?"

"Yeah, you know. I'm on all these pills now. Can't eat the foods I want—your mom changed the way she cooks everything."

"I'm sorry, Baba."

"It's what I get," he said, ruefully. "I spent forty years serving cheesesteaks out of a truck, and making some for myself to eat too. My own appetite got me into this mess."

Mama walked back in, carrying a tray of lemonade and *bizir*, the dried pumpkin seeds that she salts and bakes herself. I served my father, grabbed a handful for myself, and began cracking them between my teeth.

"Good, no?" Mama asked. "I put some in a bag. You take them home."

"OK, thanks." I shifted Michael while I popped seeds into my mouth.

"Where you live now?" Mama asked.

"At the house on 38th Street."

"With Aliyah?"

"Yes." She knew, of course, from Auntie Lamis. But she did not want to sound like she was checking on me.

"What you doing for money?"

"Actually, I'm selling some of my crafts. That way I can stay home with Michael."

"He don't give you money, that John?"

"He does, but I don't want to take it."

She didn't say anything, but I could tell she was pleased, somehow, by this.

"What you sell?"

"The baskets that you taught me how to make. I'm selling a lot, and making a lot of money," I lied.

Her smile spread across her face like a rose's petals unfolding. "That's good. You a smart girl."

"Thanks."

"That's what I tell Lamis. I tell her, *ya* Imm Nabeel, Hanan maybe she don't listen, but she smart."

"I see."

"So, John, he leaved you the house? Even after he walk out and divorced you?"

"We're not actually divorced yet. And John still comes to visit us, once a week. When Michael gets older, we'll share him on the weekends and summers."

"You let him back into your house? After what he do—"

"Mama," I interrupted sharply. "It's *his* house. He pays the mortgage. He did even when we were married, because he made more money than I did."

"Well, why did you get married? I tell you why. Because he tricked you, that man. That's what I always tell Imm Nabeel."

"What is Lamis saying?"

"She's mad why Aliyah is moving in with you. It's not proper, she says. Maybe she think that man, he trick Aliyah too."

"You know what, Mama?" I said tiredly. "Nobody tricked me. I did what I did because I wanted to." I stood up and started putting Michael back into his carseat.

"Hanan! Where are you going?"

"Look, I'm not doing so great right now. I know that, but I don't need to hear it from you. I really don't."

"If you hear me before, you don't get into these problem," she answered in a wild tone, her hand slamming down hard on the coffee table, rattling the dish of bizir.

Baba implored me to stay, but I left anyway. I kissed him goodbye at the door. His eyes were red and weary, and he said, "Hanan, don't let this keep you away." I promised to try, but I didn't look him in the eyes.

Two days after the yard sale, I returned with Michael to the Cabbages and Kings gift shop on Walnut Street. Anne had a Christmas display set up in the window, fake white snow painted onto the glass, framing a Santa and Mrs. Claus designed out of stuffed, velvet pillows.

"Nice display, Anne," I said, walking in and seeing her kneeling before a wooden trunk filled with ornaments. She was arranging them inside according to color and shape. Some were painted glass, while others were made of embroidered felt.

"Hi there!" She rose and pinched Michael's cheek gently. "Christmas in July."

"Not sure if you remember me, Anne, but I was here . . ."

"Sure, I do. Hanan, right?" She pronounced my name perfectly, which threw me off for a second.

"Right. You pronounced that very well."

"I have a friend from Lebanon. I told him I'd met a young Palestinian woman, and I tried to pronounce your name. He basically helped me not to butcher it."

"Well, it's nice to hear it pronounced correctly."

"How've you been?" She walked back behind the counter and started arranging some flyers and small knickknacks along its surface.

"OK. I wanted to tell you that I've been attending some craft shows lately, selling my baskets."

"How many have you sold so far?"

"Well, I've only done three shows, but I've sold twenty baskets." That was a lie, and I felt horrible for telling it. I'd only done two shows and sold eleven baskets, but I had made over three hundred dollars, and I had an idea for how to make more.

I tried to sound casual and nonchalant. "I was wondering if perhaps you'd be interested in selling some of my baskets here in the store. I thought people would like them—like I said, I've done well at these craft shows—and we could split the profits."

She paused and thought to herself. "How much do you sell them for?"

"Between twenty-five and thirty-five dollars. Sometimes fifty for the big ones."

"I don't pay unless they sell. And I would take 20 percent of the profits, whatever does sell."

"And you would just let me know when to come up and replenish the stock."

"What about orders? Could customers take orders?"

"Sure—I'd fill the orders in a week or less."

"I like the idea," she said pensively. "But I'd have to see some of these baskets first."

"Well . . ." I pulled out a plastic bag from underneath Michael's stroller.

"You've come prepared."

"Of course." I grinned, and she smiled back, winking at me.

I'd brought two baskets, one small and one large. The small one, the size of a dinner plate but deeper, was red and dark brown, with a braided pattern. The large one was as round as a pasta bowl, deep, and brown and beige in its pattern, with some gold thread weaved through to create a glinting reflection.

"These are stunning," Anne said simply. "You have a deal."

I had promised Baba not to stay away, and I did my best to keep it. On a late August day, I drove with Michael down to South Philly again, getting off the expressway and navigating carefully through the tight streets. Michael gurgled in the backseat, and I checked his face in the mirror I had posted on the back headrest. He had to face the rear, so that was the only way I could keep an eye on him. As I waited at a stop sign, I looked again. "We're going to visit your grandpa,

Michael. Your *sido*," I said in my merriest voice. I saw my son's reflection smile.

Baba was waiting for me at the front door as usual. When he saw me approach, he hurried out and waved at me to stop while he removed two chairs from the parking spot he'd saved. I laughed and gave him a thumbs-up sign while I parallel-parked smoothly into the space.

He hugged me tightly when I got out, and I couldn't help noticing how thin his arms had become. I handed him Michael's carseat to carry while I lugged the heavy kitchen chairs inside the house.

"Your mother went to the store to do some grocery shopping," he said apologetically. I nodded, but I knew he was lying.

"I'll make us some iced tea," he said, but I stopped him from getting out of his chair.

"I'll make it," I explained calmly, as I took Michael out of his seat and placed him gently in my father's arms. "Michael came to spend some time with his *sido*."

While I stood at the kitchen counter, mixing the sugary iced tea powder into a jug of cool water, I listened to my father make gurgling noises to Michael, then sing little ditties quietly to him. I stirred slowly on purpose, taking my time, looking around the kitchen.

It hadn't changed much since I was a child. The faux oak cabinets hung over the bright yellow formica countertops, and despite their age, they were in perfect condition. I checked the side counter next to the sink and, yes, the scratch mark was still there. I had once etched the counter as a kid with Mama's keys, dragging a long, sleek line through the formica's yellow surface, exposing the white plastic beneath. Mama had painted it carefully with yellow paint so that it would not show, and she made it a point to touch up the paint every few months. Even the linoleum on the floor had never been changed, but despite the areas where it had become worn down, it shone with cleanliness and sparkled with careful attention.

"Baba, don't you guys think it's time to update the kitchen a bit?" I asked, carrying two glasses back into the living room.

"I wish!" he said, looking up from Michael's face. "But you know your mother."

Mama had refused to replace anything that still worked or served its purpose. I knew that the cushions on the couch were worn out on the underside. Once the maroon velour on top wore out as well, it might be time to talk about a new set. But she still complained that leaving the plastic covers on would have preserved it forever.

"It's the mentality left over from how she grew up," Baba said. "From the camps, you know how life was there." He rocked Michael gently, and I saw my son rub his eyes sleepily.

"He'll be out soon," I said. "Keep rocking him . . . It's time for his nap soon anyway." We sat quietly together, watching Michael drift off to sleep, his eyelids fluttering as he tried valiantly to ward off his drowsiness. When he finally succumbed, I went to put him back in his carseat, but Baba wouldn't let me. "I'll hold him . . . it's OK."

"He looks like our family, doesn't he?"

"His eyes are dark like ours. And his fingers are shaped like mine, I think." Baba picked up Michael's left hand and studied it. I moved closer to see. He was right—Michael's fingers were long, but wider at the base and then tapering down to the fingernails. Baba's hands were the same, like isosceles triangles.

"You know my father's hands were like this too."

I looked at my own fingers, which were shorter and slim, the fingertips squared. Like my mother's.

"I wish I'd known him," I said. "And Siti too."

"Well, he died in '74, not long after your grandmother." Baba settled into his chair and leaned his head back. "The men overseas—they depend so much on their wives. If the woman dies first, everyone says the husband will follow soon. And he usually does."

"Really?" I asked skeptically, thinking that of all the couples I knew, most of the men seemed like they would live longer if their wives went first. The quality of life might improve drastically.

"Oh, the women are the strong ones," he said, nodding. "They keep the house together, the family together. My parents came to America in 1944, but then they went back in the 1960s—once I was eighteen, actually."

"Why didn't they stay?"

"They had land they wanted to protect—it was a bad time. Land was being snatched, and everyone was worried that if they stayed away, they'd have nothing left when they went home."

He took a sip of his iced tea, then added, "Home is everything." I looked down, away from his eyes.

"Did I ever tell you about when your grandfather was kidnapped by the Ottomans?" he asked brightly, deliberately changing the subject. I shook my head.

"During World War I, the Ottomans were under attack by the British, the French, everyone," he began. "And their army was losing so they used to come to the villages and take the young men, draft them into the army, and make them fight. Usually those men died or they were just never seen again."

"When they came to our village, they kidnapped over two hundred boys and men. My grandmother tried to hide my father, in the wheat stacks under the farmhouse. But they knew a young man lived in that house, and they threatened to kill the whole family if they didn't produce him. My father gave himself up."

"They tied his hands to a long rope, to the back of a horse, with others, like a chain of prisoners, and dragged him off. He ended up in Damascus, in a battle camp, training to fight. He learned to engage in combat, ride a horse, handle a sword. But then the war ended—it was over, and he was stranded in Syria, alone."

He paused a few moments. "Do you know what he did?"

I waited intently.

"He walked home." He paused again for effect. "Yes, he walked home from Syria to our village in Palestine. He knew Palestine was southwest of Syria, so he followed the sun until he reached the Jordan River, then he followed it south. He slept at night wherever he could, in fields and hiding out in orchards. At one point, he met up with a band of Bedouins, and he spent two months traveling with them."

"How long did it take him?" "The journey home was long—it took him almost two full years. His family was shocked. It was like he'd returned from the dead."

I imagined my grandfather, whom I'd only seen in a few sepia-toned photographs, arriving at his parents' home, dusty, perhaps with long hair and a full, disheveled beard. Would they have recognized him at first? What did his mother do when she finally realized it was her son, and not a beggar, on the front step?

"I can't believe I never heard that story before," I said to Baba. "I'm glad you told me."

"There are many stories," he replied. "And I want Michael to hear them all."

When the phone rang at half past midnight, I was awake, nursing Michael. He woke several times at night, usually every two to three hours, wailing in hunger, so I'd learned to adjust my sleep pattern as well. Afraid it would wake Aliyah, who'd gone to sleep late, I deftly snatched the phone with my left hand, supporting Michael's head with my right. The receiver was on the table beside my bed, and I had to dodge the pacifier, tub of baby wipes, and dirty bibs that littered its surface.

"Hanan? It's me." My mother sounded frantic.

"What's wrong? Is Baba OK?"

"We're in the St. Agnes. He have heart attack."

Aliyah offered to keep Michael with her, but I took him anyway, strapping him into the carseat in his pajamas. He was screaming because I'd interrupted his feeding session, but he quieted down as the car's motion lulled him back to sleep.

I gave the car to the valet parking service and hurried inside, pushing Michael along in the stroller. My mother was waiting in the lobby, and we took the elevator up to the intensive care unit. We didn't say a word, but I was tapping my foot nervously, and, in a simple, swift motion, she took my hand in her own and held it until we reached the fifth floor.

My father was heavily sedated. He looked pale, washed out, especially in a white gown lying in a bed of white sheets. A tube had been inserted in his throat, and a monitor tracked his heart rate. It beeped incessantly, scaring me, even though I knew it was communicating to me that my father was doing well, that his heart was beating steadily.

"He woke up and he can't breathe," my mother explained. "His chest hurt, his left side, and I think, oh my God, not now, please. I called the 911, and they come so fast, but I do the CPR thing anyway. When they come, they tell me I did good job, and then they take him. I only stopped to take your number with me."

"You did CPR?"

"Yes. It helped, because he really stop breathing."

"How did you know how to do CPR?"

"I take the course, after he in the hospital last time. They make me practice on the big doll."

"I can't believe you learned CPR."

"It's easy," she said dismissively. "Look—Michael."

I looked down at him, and indeed he was awake, wide-eyed, staring at us. "Oh, I didn't even realize—"

"Shhh . . ." she said softly.

"He's probably hungry. He'll start crying in a minute."

"No, no, he's sleeping." She rocked the stroller back and forth gently, and his eyelids dropped down slowly upon his cheeks.

"You used to do that, when you were baby. You open your eyes in the sleep, so you look awake, but still asleep."

I sat down on the long, vinyl-upholstered bench in the corner. "He still wakes up every night, at least two or three times, to eat."

"Soon he will sleep long. You start sleeping long when you were six months. So he have time."

"I'm adjusting, but I'm still tired all the time," I confessed to her.

"Because you do it by yourself. You should not do by yourself."

Suddenly, I wanted to cry. Exhausted and irritable, I wondered why on earth I was doing this by myself. How had I ended up raising a child on my own?

"I don't know how it happened this way."

"Because you stubborn." When I looked up at her, ready to say something, she quickly added, "Like me. You just like me, Hanan. Is this so bad?"

I didn't answer. I didn't know what to say to her.

The nurse walked in then and checked my father's vital signs. "Looking good," she said to us. "The doctor will be in soon to check on him."

"Thank you," I said.

"We have some coffee behind the nurses' station, if you like," she said to us. "The cafeteria upstairs won't open for another few hours."

"OK, " I said. I offered to get some for my mom and myself.

"No, I get it. I stay awake with Baba and the baby. You sleep."

"No, I'm fine . . ." I started to protest.

"You tired, Hanan. You have to sleep."

She left and returned a few minutes later with a large paper cup in her hand. "This American coffee so disgusting. It tastes like dirty water," she said. "American people—they drink coffee only to stay awake. Not to enjoy it."

I curled up on the large chair next to Baba's bed. "It's not so bad," I said. "I'm just closing my eyes for a few minutes, OK."

"OK. You sleep, *habibti*. I'm here now."

REEMA

Chasing Valentino

It wasn't until Alex started asking about polygamy that Reema got worried. He asked with a hesitant, desperately curious expression on his face: the slight arching of the left brow, the slightly audible intake of breath as he leaned forward. She'd known it would eventually come, but did not expect it at Marian's Café on Market Street on a Saturday that had started so beautifully.

"Isn't it true that Arabian men can marry four women? That Islam permits men to have harems . . . and seraglios?" She intuitively knew that he added that last word to polish off the question with an intellectual coat of wax. At least he had the grace to look modest.

"Well," Reema began, lowering her voice so that the other clientele in the café wouldn't hear, "Muslim men can technically marry four women, according to the Koran, but they don't really do that anymore. And harems are a thing of the past." She suddenly wished she hadn't been available when he called that morning. How innocent he had sounded a mere four hours ago.

"But doesn't that affect you—or bother you—as a feminist?"

"There are a lot of historical reasons for it. It's not reducible to sexism." She hoped her tone sounded final. But his narrowed eyes told her the truth: He thought she was apologizing for her culture the way that you apologize to your party guests for the burned roast and a flopped soufflé.

Alex didn't speak, which suited her mood just fine. They paid the bill and strolled through the dusky Philadelphia streets, arm in arm. A show was just letting out of the Walnut Street Theatre, and she made a mental note to check their showbill for the upcoming week. She hadn't been to a show in ages.

She'd met him six weeks ago through Aliyah's brother Nabeel. Nabeel and Alex worked together at an antiques gallery on Market Street, and since she lived only one block from there, Nabeel invited her to meet them for lunch one day.

Over the meal, Nabeel had teased her. "Aliyah said to tell you she and the other girls are mad at you." Reema blushed: she hadn't seen Nabeel's sister, or Hanan and Nadia, in months. Everyone knew that Reema wasn't doing much over the summer in terms of "real" work. She was in the final two years of the PhD, progressing with her dissertation—a collection and study of eyewitness accounts of war. It had reached one hundred and four pages by the end of June, when Nabeel called her for lunch. June 16th, in fact. She remembered the date because she hadn't touched the dissertation, or any of the books stacked beside her desk, since then.

Now she spent all her time with Alex. Even when she wasn't with him, she found herself too high-strung to actually sit down and shape the draft. The words had simply lumped on the pages, unformed and incoherent, but she lacked the strength these days to chisel them into significance. Should she focus on just the stories of women, or of all war survivors? Should their stories be left "as is," or incorporated into the historical context? And what about tracking people down?

Her NGO connections did not seem to be panning out, no matter how many emails she composed and sent. The dissertation was spinning out of control, and her advisor would not be happy at next month's update meeting.

However, all thoughts of it disappeared when she was around Alex. At 6 feet 3 inches, he had to lean down to kiss her, and it seemed as if his arms could wrap around her twice. He had pale blue eyes, flecked with a deeper blue, and his black hair was long and curly, flapping behind his ears like raven's wings.

When she first saw him with Nabeel, he'd paused before saying "Hello," and she sensed the attraction. Like the "thunderbolt," Michael Corleone experiences in *The Godfather*, or the "seizing of the heart" her own grandfather used to say he felt upon meeting her grandmother. She could not suppress her smiles, and she felt goofy and sexy all at once.

"I can't believe Nabeel didn't introduce him to *me*. Bastard," Aliyah said.

Reema sat on the couch of her apartment with a bottle of glittery copper polish, her feet on the coffee table. She had called Aliyah after such a long time to talk about Alex, and it felt good to share secrets again, like they had when they were little. "Well, Nabeel has always thought of me as his sister too, you know," she teased.

"*Habibti!* Is that right?"

They giggled like schoolgirls again for a long time, enjoying their togetherness. The last time they had been close, acting like silly teenagers, was years ago, when Aliyah had moved out of her parents' house and needed help decorating—the result had been lilac walls, sofas with originally designed and stitched flowered slipcovers, and a kitchen table painted in a black and white checkerboard pattern. All their mothers had collectively frowned, worrying that Aliyah's show of independence would have a domino effect. On Reema, it had.

On her first date with Alex, they met at the Lebanese café on 9th Street, managed by an elderly, slim man, his sons, and their wives for as long as Reema could remember. Over hummus and lemon chicken kabobs, Reema told Alex how she'd been pulled into sociology. "I want to study the culture created by war, and examine how victims cope in new worlds. My interest is really coming out of the fact that my parents are refugees of war and immigrants to the States—I have no doubt about that."

"I just sell antiques," he said as he walked her home later than night. "That's all I could find with an art history degree."

"You don't enjoy it?"

"I love antiques and old things, but the job basically sucks." Then he kissed her, right there at the front door of her building. Tenderly. Sweetly. She called Aliyah that night for the first time in months, and they stayed on the phone until 2 A.M.

She continued to see Alex, almost every night of the week, and they quickly fell into a routine: He walked over to her apartment after work, where they ate dinner (he insisted that she cook Middle Eastern food, so rolling grape leaves, not her thesis, occupied the daytime hours). After dinner, they watched one of the prime-time sitcoms, usually *Seinfeld* or *Frasier*, or the reruns of *Cheers* if they were so lucky. Then they'd take a walk for at least an hour, strolling through the marvellously organized grid of streets that defined Philadelphia. Numbers running north and south; names going east and west. One-way streets, no deviations. It was comforting for the same reason that arithmetic always appealed to her in school—there was only *one* answer, just waiting to be discovered.

She loved the way he spoke, the way that he compressed his lips after making a point. "I'm a film buff," he said once, a few weeks after the disturbing polygamy question. "I collect old movies. I think you'd like them," his mouth engulfing the final "m" and sealing it in.

"What's the oldest movie you own?" she asked.

"*The Sheik*, made in 1921." He grinned. "You'd *love* that one."

"What's it about?"

"It's a Rudolph Valentino classic." They approached City Hall, which squatted at the intersection of Market and Broad Streets—solid, square, its white stone carved with figures that formed a Pantheon-like facade. They passed through the Market Street entrance to the building's central courtyard, where the moon shone down on the sundial etched on the floor. They sat on a small ledge, off to the side, holding hands.

"It's the movie that made his career," Alex continued. "A silent movie, where this desert sheik lusts after an English girl and kidnaps her. He keeps her in his tent and basically makes her his sex slave, although it's not as obvious as that. It turns out well," he reassured her. "They actually fall in love at the end."

"Fall in love? After he's kidnapped her?" She dismissed it as a cheesy romance fluff novel plot, but Alex brought the film to her apartment the next night. She had made *tabouleh*, another of Alex's favorites. It had consumed most of her afternoon, chopping the tomatoes, parsley, and onions into the seedling-size proportions required by the recipe. She served it with mint tea, for which Alex kissed her hand and declared that he was "in paradise with a houri."

"You're crazy," she said, laughing. "Let's watch the movie."

Chagrined, he asked, "A good Muslim man gets seventy houris in heaven, right?"

"I guess."

"So what does a good Muslim woman get? Like, what will *you* get in heaven?"

She answered wearily, "I get to be somebody's houri?"

He pushed the play button and fell onto the couch next to her. He kissed her deeply, and pushed his hand into her hair. When he pulled away, he gazed down at her, his voice ragged this time. "You're *my* houri."

She only pondered those words when she and Alex were well into the film. Valentino, wearing a turban and a white cloak, crept stealthily and lustfully toward the unsuspecting Agnes Ayres, who wept for her stolen freedom in a corner of his tent. "Watch his face when he sees her crying," whispered Alex.

Rudolph's face crumpled, dissolved from lust to guilt and shame. Reema glanced at Alex's face in the semidarkness: entranced, fixed on the scene, as if he were Valentino himself, suffering a sudden pang of conscience that he'd terrified this beautiful woman.

"How many times have you seen this film?"

"At least twenty times. I know every scene."

When it was over, he wanted her opinion. "You're an Arabian," he prefaced.

"Arab."

"Arab. Sorry. What's your take?"

What could she say to him? That she was somewhat offended by it? That it was full of stereotypes? She tried to express this tactfully, so as not to hurt his feelings.

"You must be kidding."

"Alex, it's horribly racist. Why is there not one decent Arab in the whole movie?"

"What about the Sheik himself—Valentino?"

"He turns out to be half Spanish and half English—not a coincidence, I'm sure."

"But he's raised in an Arab *culture*. He's an orphan and—"

"Oh, Alex—men who kidnap women or buy them at bride auctions? That's Arab culture? Come *on*."

He didn't respond.

"You know that's racist, don't you? They didn't understand Arab culture then."

"Of course I know that." He kissed her hand and said, "Let's forget it. We can agree to disagree."

She didn't see *how* he could agree to disagree, because you cannot disagree about something that's incorrect. You could never say, for example, "I just don't believe in a heliocentric view of the universe, but we can agree to disagree." But she dropped it, because there's always a time period in a relationship, usually toward the beginning, when people accept anything, when nothing is enough to make into a big deal. She kept quiet even when they had dinner with his friends for the first time and he introduced her as Reema, his "beautiful harem girl" to elicit a laugh and break the ice. When he asked her to tell him stories of her childhood, about her parents and their idiosyncrasies, about her brother and how he'd met his wife during a two-week vacation to Palestine, and then said that he felt like Sultan Shahrayar of the *Thousand and One Nights*—which Reema supposed made her like Scheherazade. She just kept reminding herself of how blue his eyes were.

Since she had been old enough to understand it, she'd been bothered by the fact that people told her that she looked "exotic" (which, until the age of fourteen, she'd confused with "erotic"). The clerk at the post office, the police officer who'd stopped her for running a red light, people at school, such as the classmate who'd insisted that the shape and darkness of her eyes made him imagine "what Cleopatra must have looked like." It was all very silly—but she tolerated it because it never seemed appropriate to be offended.

"We've all gone through stuff like that," Aliyah told her one day. "I hate it when white guys tell me I'm 'mysterious' or something like that. It's different once they get to know you."

"But Alex keeps saying that stuff. It gets worse and worse."

"That's weird," Aliyah agreed. "On the other hand, he's really nice . . . and handsome."

Reema knew that was one major consideration, despite her most logical attempts to argue with herself. But the truth was it felt good to be with someone like Alex, someone she thought would never be interested in her. Someone who wasn't scared of her culture, hesitant about leaping into something completely different.

And if Alex had false impressions of her, well then was she any better? She confessed to herself that it felt dangerous to be with Alex, too—her mother expected her to eventually marry an Arab man. But what if Alex was the one for her? She needed to break out of the box, to find out, to imagine different endings to the story her mother had scripted.

So she didn't say much about her feelings to him—in a way, she was grateful that he showed interest in her culture. There were times when she lacked interest in her Arab-ness, when she wanted it to disappear and just wake up blonde and green-eyed, with a live-in, stockbroker boyfriend who watched football on Sundays while she read *Time* magazine on the couch beside him.

That, of course, had been her parents' first rule. They didn't support her moving out in the first place ("It's not *safe*," her mother had said), but they expressly clarified that they would be compelled to disown her if it turned out that she was "with a man" or causing people to label her "*bint al haram.*"

But leaving had become necessary—not to live with a man, but to prevent the competition of cultures from fogging the path of her future. There were times when it had, when she'd hated her mother and father—their sad faces, their accents, the way they always spoke wistfully of home, as much as she felt awkward around co-workers who couldn't wait for Fridays but trudged in with Monday morning hangovers.

"Would your parents like me?" Alex asked her one night, as they took one of their nightly strolls. They headed toward South Street this time to do some window shopping and people-watching.

"I'm sure they would," Reema answered, squeezing his hand reassuringly.

"Even though I'm not an Arab?" he stared at her eagerly.

"Why do you say that?" she asked, not sure how to give him an answer. His eyes looked almost desperate.

"I mean, would they want you to be with me or with an Arab guy, like Nabeel?"

"Most parents want their children to marry within their culture—it's natural."

"So they wouldn't like me?"

"I'm not saying that."

"Yes, you are." He dropped her hand. "They probably wouldn't even like you being with me. I'm disgracing the family or some crap like that and then your brother would have to kill you to preserve everyone's honor."

"Oh, don't be ridiculous," she snapped. "And have you told your parents about *me*?" she counterattacked. "What did they say?"

He stopped under a street lamp, and she could see an odd smile on his lips. "Actually, I mentioned you to my mother and—goddamn it if she didn't ask me what color you were." He peered at her. "Isn't that weird?" The cage of his mouth swallowed the "d."

"She asked you *what*?"

"I told her that I was dating you, and she asked me what your name was. I said, 'Reema,' and she asked what you were. You know, like what nationality. When I said that you were Arab, she asked what color you were."

Reema wondered how her face looked to Alex at that moment, illuminated by the lamplight. How did her skin look against the red wool of her coat, the white of her scarf? Did she resemble Agnes Ayres, gazing up at Valentino in his white turban, flashing a maniacal smile? Reema briefly considered clasping her hands together in a helpless gesture, and raising her eyes heavenward in a silent prayer for the preservation of her purity.

"And what did she do when you told her that I was—what? How did you say it?—a light brown? Dark olive? What? Was she relieved?"

He hesitated, then said, "I told her that you were the most beautiful woman in the world, and that she'd be as enchanted with you as I am."

And Reema was certain she never wanted to meet his mother.

They continued to walk, had their fill of people-watching, and headed back to Reema's apartment. She hoped that he would leave right away—her head was spinning and she needed to think—but from the way that he stroked her hair as she fiddled with the key, she knew that he planned to stay a while.

Starting to pull off her coat, she simultaneously headed for the kitchen to do the dishes, hoping that it would kill his notions, but he pulled her toward the couch instead.

"Sit down," he commanded gently. When she did, he lifted her legs onto the cushions and opened her coat so that it formed a red pillow around her. He pulled her arms free and pushed the red wool up against her breasts.

"You're tense," he declared.

"I'm not."

He began to rub her temples anyway, but the bun into which she'd pulled her hair obstructed that. He uncoiled the tightly-wound band and untwisted her hair, letting it fall around her face. She moved to brush a strand out of her eye, but he stayed her hand and settled it on the back cushion. "Let me," he said, moving the strand away from her eye, but laying it along her cheek instead, curved slightly toward her mouth. Another strand pulled out and placed like Cleopatra's asp along her breast (she knew that's what he was imagining). A heavier section of her hair arranged so that it tumbled off the side of the couch in a black wave.

He lifted her left knee slightly, stood back and observed his work, and then lowered the angle that her leg had formed.

"You're perfect," he proclaimed, satisfied like Matisse, who must have occasionally sat back from his odalisque paintings once in a while and murmured, "*Goddamn*, that's good."

Grasping the back of the couch for leverage, Reema pulled herself upright and stood up, out of his portrait.

"Please leave."

"What's wrong?"

"I want you to leave now. Please."

He stood at the door, looking confused. "Can I call you later? Then will you tell me what's wrong?"

"Maybe."

When the door closed behind him, she walked over to her window, which faced Chestnut Street below. She opened it and curled up on the wide sill. Switching on the small lamp next to the window, she waited for him to appear.

He did—hands stuffed in his pockets, head down as he walked down the street. Feeling guilty, she almost called him back. Just then, he turned around and stopped, startled, when he saw her gazing down at him from three stories up. He took his hands out of his pockets, letting them hang at his sides like pendulums, swinging ever so slightly back and forth at mid-thigh, his face upturned. She suddenly realized what sort of image she presented, framed as she was in the window, illuminated by the feeble light of the lamp. Hair down. Red coat hanging around her shoulders. She reached over, clicked off the lamp, and closed the curtains.

She fell right into bed, still wearing her coat, and woke up before dawn. Sliding on her most worn pair of jeans, she went to the university campus. She lugged her backpack up Locust Walk, lined with gnarled trees and stately brick buildings, and sat under the statue of Ben Franklin on the quad until Van Pelt Library opened. Inside, she searched carefully for the right place before claiming a table in the reading room. Her laptop screen glared before her eyes for a long time, she tapped restlessly on the keys, her brain would not settle, but still she waited for the words to come.

Intervention

Reema was becoming a collector of stories, something she'd always imagined Aliyah would do instead. But as her childhood friend reminded her, "I invent stories, for the most part. You record them." And there was one story in particular that Reema was determined to acquire.

She consulted Aliyah and Hanan first, and they supported her decision. So she called Nadia and set up the interview.

"But I thought your thesis was on immigrant women," Nadia initially responded. It had been, Reema lied, but her advisor had suggested expanding her scope to the children of immigrants and their experiences with assimilation.

"Sure, let's do it," Nadia agreed, and invited her over the next evening. Reema spent the rest of the night plotting how things would progress, wondering if the conversation would proceed the way she hoped.

Of all her friends, she knew Nadia the least. She'd met Aliyah first, when they were both students at the Catholic school in the neighborhood. Reema had never felt like an outsider until the fifth grade, when her aunt, who was visiting from the West Bank, showed up with her mother to pick her up after school. It was meant to be a surprise, but it changed everything.

As Reema walked out of the classroom building, in single file behind her classmates, she sensed the commotion in the courtyard. Several students gasped and giggled, while others just stared at some point at the end of the blacktop. She saw her math teacher, a tall angular woman with long, red hair, roll her eyes and walk huffily back into the building.

Reema's eyes followed the direction in which her classmates were pointing, and there was her aunt, standing by the fence next to the tetherball pole. A sickening wave flooded Reema's stomach as she realized her aunt was wearing her white hijab. Of course, she knew this—she'd seen her aunt every day this week—but she suddenly imagined how her aunt must appear to her classmates.

"Who's that?" she heard people—mothers and children—whisper to each other.

"That's my aunt," she said fiercely to nobody in particular, then walked over stiffly. During the three-block walk home, her mother and aunt chatted easily while Reema hugged the straps of her backpack closer to the center of her chest. She avoided looking across the street, where two of her friends were walking home with their own mothers. Cars passed between them, offering Reema a temporary reprieve from their stares.

The next day in school was the first time anyone called her a "towelhead"—she felt like she had been slapped in the face. Aliyah approached her after that, stayed close by, even though she was in the seventh grade, two whole years older. Before the Christmas break, they were both towelheads, and by the end of the year, Nadia and Hanan had joined their camel jockey circle.

Hanan's thoughts usually poured forth from her lips. She showed her love with passion and demonstrated her hate with rage. Once, when an eighth-grade boy called her "sand eater," she punched him in the face, knocking him to the ground. "I guess you're eating it now," she tossed back. Nadia was more reserved, her face a pleasant mask she rarely removed. Lately that mask had been firmly fixed, opaque, impossible to penetrate. She was brave, not openly like Hanan, but in her own, subtle way.

Nadia opened the door and greeted her with a kiss on each cheek. "Come in—I haven't seen you in such a long time!"

"We've both been busy, I'm sure."

"Yes, but that's no excuse." Nadia walked ahead of her to the living room, and Reema noticed her gait had resumed much of its natural grace.

"You seem like you're doing really well, Nadia. I'm happy to see that." She kicked off her shoes, as she was used to doing in Nadia's apartment, and sat cross-legged on the couch. The living room was small, with shiny hardwood floors and sofas in beige damask. A hand-embroidered afghan and brightly embroidered pillows decorated every sofa and chair in the small room, lending it a pleasant and intimate atmosphere.

"Thanks. I'm feeling better every day. Back to work now five days a week." She offered to make coffee or tea, but Reema asked instead for a glass of water. Nadia brought back a tray with two glasses, a small pecan cake, a serving knife, forks and delicate pink plates. "I hope you have an appetite for one of my mom's pastries. She just experimented with this last night, and I couldn't wait to try it."

"Oh, I always have room for Auntie Siham's cooking, baking, anything!"

When they finished their cake and were chatting easily, Nadia asked, "How should we begin this? I mean, do you want to tape the conversation, take notes . . . ?"

Reema, who had not brought anything with her except her purse, shook her head slowly. "Actually, Nadia, I wasn't honest with you on the phone." She paused.

"OK?"

"We're like sisters, right?"

"Of course!"

"Well, sisters are different than friends." Reema took a sip of her water. She'd rehearsed this little opening speech last night carefully. "Because sisters are obligated to tell each other when they are doing something that is hurtful or detrimental. Friends would probably do the same thing, but it's not obligatory . . ."

"Reema? What's going on?" Nadia leaned forward, off the couch, planting both feet on the floor.

"George may be getting married."

"Was Siham home?" Mama asked when she stopped home for dinner that night. She spoke in Arabic, as she had done since Reema was a little girl. Now all their conversations were in Arabic. Reema conversed in it comfortably, switching between it and English as easily as changing her shirt or her shoes.

"No, I didn't see her. Only Nadia was there." She walked over to the stove and, at her mother's instructive nod, stirred the onions that simmered in the oil. Her mother was cooking *majaddarah*, one of the simplest meals, really—it only consisted of rice and lentils, but it was one of Reema's favorites. Actually, everything Mama made was delicious, and she secretly felt that her mother was a superior cook to the other mothers.

"Not too long, Reema. They'll turn black very quickly."

She scooped them out with a spatula and let them drain on a paper towel laid over a plate. Then her mother took the tiny amount of oil and poured it into the larger pot, where she mixed it in thoroughly with the rice and lentils. "That's my secret," she said with a wink. "It gives it great flavor."

"You tell me as if I'll ever be as good of a cook as you are."

"You will be better in cooking and in many other things than I am, *insha'allah*." She set the *majaddarah* in the center of the table and reaching for the onions. "Call your brothers so we can eat."

"Before I do," Reema said simply, "I need your advice."

Her mother glanced up at her face, recognized its seriousness, and sat down obediently, expectantly, on a kitchen chair.

Reema sat down as well, and spoke slowly. "First of all, you cannot say anything about this to anyone, not even Auntie Layla or Imm Nabeel . . ."

"Of course not—don't let it concern you."

"You know that, last year, Nadia broke up with George."

"Yes. Siham never gave a reason."

"Well, today I found out why."

"The accident? God help her and her mother, she suffered terribly, but she cannot blame him."

"It's worse." Reema told her mother about the invisible damage the accident had rendered to Nadia's body, about how her uterus had been ruptured and would never allow her to carry a fetus to full-term. She spoke calmly, not looking up at her mother's face until she was finished. When she finally did, she was shocked to see her mother weeping silently, large, full teardrops streaking down her cheeks.

"Oh, God help us, God help us . . ."

"I didn't mean to upset you."

"I'm more upset that Siham and her daughter have been suffering like this—without anyone's knowledge. It's been so long since the accident—nobody knew!"

Reema reminded her mother that they didn't want anyone to know, especially George. And yet, there was the problem. George, since the breakup, had refused to give up on Nadia, hoping she was going through a bout of depression because of the accident, a cloud that would eventually lift and pass on.

"I swore to Nadia I wouldn't tell anyone," Reema confided in her mother. "But I feel like George should know. I heard his parents are pressuring him to marry a girl, a friend of their family, and he is thinking of just doing that. Nadia isn't giving him any hope, after all."

Her mother remained silent for several seconds, then said, with a tone of finality, "He deserves to know."

"But Nadia? She'll kill me."

Mama shook her head, as if to erase a nagging thought. "You have to tell him. When you tell the truth, you allow people the chance to heal."

"What if it doesn't make a difference?"

"Don't be afraid. It will."

Reema went for a jog one early morning along Boathouse Row to clear her mind. Two of the boating clubs were out on the water, pulling their oars back and forth in synchronous movements, cutting through the water gracefully but powerfully. They moved as one unit, not one person disturbing the quiet rhythm they had generated together. She kept her eyes on them until they went under the bridge and then out of sight.

She hadn't been jogging in several months, not since her dissertation research had begun in earnest. Her endurance had certainly suffered from a lack of practice, as now she found herself panting from having completed a small hill, one that she had, in the past, accomplished without having noticed the incline of the road.

Her slower pace allowed her ample time to think, to remember her dilemma. "My mother is right," Nadia had told her that night in her apartment. "George is an only son, and his parents would not let him marry me, knowing the situation."

"But don't you think he should know about it? He doesn't have a clue why you stopped talking to him."

She shrugged. "He'll forget me eventually. Besides how could I put him in that situation? I know he loves children."

Reema was struck by Nadia's woeful tone, but also by her sense of righteousness. She truly believed she was somehow saving George from a lifetime of sorrow by pushing him away, by ending it.

"What does that mean then?" she'd asked her. "Do you think you somehow don't 'deserve' to be married to someone you love because you might have troubling having children?"

Nadia had only shrugged, and Reema had suddenly been struck by a painful thought—"She really doesn't care about herself at all."

"Nadia, he loves you."

"Reema," she had said wearily. "I don't know what else to say to you. I wish I hadn't said anything at all. It's over, and I'll be fine—don't worry. We can't change anything."

Reema turned and headed back toward the Benjamin Franklin Parkway, the way she had come, to return to her apartment. As she ran, forcing herself to push off her heel smoothly into the next step, she felt her breath coming back, filling her lungs, and the old exuberance she used to have as an undergraduate, when she ran every other day with her customary "long run" on Sundays.

To her right, out of the corner of her eye, she glimpsed the rowing team returning across the river. This time she stopped, moved off to the side, and shielded her eyes from the sun to observe them more closely. Their arms were once again in unison, sweeping the oars back and forth, the water parting before them obediently. They were powerful, majestic, and beautiful to see.

Later that morning, when Reema stepped off the subway at 15th and Market, George was already waiting for her underneath the Clothespin. The statue, made of stainless steel, loomed forty-five feet over the major intersection, with majestic City Hall in the background.

George waved awkwardly as she approached. "Get some coffee?" he asked in Arabic.

"I'd rather just talk if you don't mind," she said, also in Arabic, "because I'm not even sure I should have called you."

He didn't reply, just sat down on a nearby bench.

She sat beside him. "I should say thanks for coming in the first place. I know it was short notice."

"No problem," he replied anxiously. "I have only a short break at work—I have surgery this afternoon—so I hope I didn't bring you out too far." He gestured toward the statue. "Nobody can miss this thing, so I thought it was the easiest place."

"Oh, of course," she replied awkwardly. "I love this statue anyway. I knew exactly what you were referring to."

"You love this thing?" He turned and looked at it again, studied it for a few seconds, then faced her. "I don't get it, I guess. Abstract art was never my favorite."

"It's brilliant."

"It's a clothespin."

"No, it's not."

He waited expectantly.

"It's two people embracing."

"What!" He turned again.

"You can't see it from this angle," she interjected quickly. "You'll have to wait until we're in front of it." Then she asked bluntly, "Are you getting married?"

His eyebrows shot up. "Well, yes. I mean no, not really." He cleared his throat. "What I should say is that my parents have asked me to consider marrying a young woman, the daughter of a friend of my father's. They think her family would be agreeable to an arrangement."

She apologized. "I didn't mean to intrude, but you need to know something about Nadia before you make that decision."

"Nadia? I haven't spoken to her in over a year. Since the accident." He crossed his arms over his chest. "You know this."

"Yes, I do."

"How is she?" he asked eagerly, leaning forward.

"She's gotten so thin—you haven't seen her—and all she does is go to work, come home, sleep, and repeat it all the next day. I don't remember the last time she went out with us, laughed, had a good time."

George frowned. "That hurts me. But what can I do?"

"What would you say," Reema said, choosing her words carefully, "if you knew Nadia still loved you?"

"Still loves me?"

"Do you still love her?"

"I do," he replied simply.

"Do you want to be a father one day?" Reema asked him.

"Of course."

"What if Nadia was not able to carry your children?" When he didn't reply, Reema felt herself panic. She started to get up, but George suddenly gave her an awful look, as if he had just awakened from a daze.

"Don't go." His voice was clipped, sharp. It was a command, not a request.

When he spoke again, his voice was forced, belabored with patience. "Reema, there is more than one way to become a father."

She didn't respond, but she watched his expression change carefully from shock to anger.

"Are you actually saying," he asked her, his voice rising, "that we have wasted *one year?*"

He walked her back to the subway station. "Should I call her?"

"I'd better call her first. She'll be furious with me, but at least I'll prepare her."

"Reema."

His tone was urgent. She stopped walking and looked up at him.

"I'm not a shallow man. If I have Nadia, that is everything. I want you to make her understand that. We'll figure out the rest later."

"I will." She pointed up, behind him. "Look at it now."

He turned and viewed the Clothespin from the front. Its slim, tall halves were transformed into two lovers, the metal spring metamorphosed into arms, holding one another close. Their faces were nearly touching, almost kissing.

"Oh yes," he said. "Yes, I see it now."

The Scent of Oranges

I don't understand why it's important, but I'll do this as you wish, Reema. I have an hour before the grape leaves finish cooking. Do you have to record? I wish you wouldn't. I'm not good at choosing my words—I have to think for hours to find the right one, but y'allah.

When the alarm sounded, its shrill wail threw me back, far back in my mind to the classroom in the UNRWA school at the east end of the camp. I shared a desk with Huda, and we used to hold each other tightly under it when the air raid sirens rang and the planes soared above. If they dropped their loads, we were sent home early, running home to our frantic mothers. If they just passed quietly overhead, we went back to our schoolwork, figuring out what x and y were in the algebraic equations, or practicing our English conversational skills: "May I have some milk in my tea? Thank you kindly." Goddamn British.

Sorry, habibti. *Be sure to erase that part later. Promise? I know you said you need accurate stories for the project—the "thesis," yes I know—but I don't want that word on there.*

So that's how we spent our schooldays. Once in a while, a bomb landed on the home of someone we knew, a person in our class, and they would stop coming to our school. We would either attend the funeral, or hear from one of the old people in town or from one of the young men who worked in the city, that our classmate was at a special school for orphans.

Let me interrupt again, Reema. Really, please be sure to go back and erase the curse word I said. Just say instead, "the meddling British"—not too easy on them, but not cursing either.

Philadelphia was strange at first. Their English here was different, and they did not put milk in their tea. I hated it, even though I was grateful to your grandfather, God rest his soul, for getting us to America. The West Bank had been swallowed up, and my father decided we couldn't wait any longer to return to Palestine.

On my first day in the new school—that's when the siren went off. In English class, the middle of the day. Mr. Emmitt was the teacher; he had black hair and thick glasses, and a gap between his front teeth, but I thought he was very handsome, even for a man without a mustache, but especially because all my teachers at the camp had been women. He seemed to smile especially at me—*why are you groaning, Reema?*—and my heart actually fluttered. I'm a woman, you know, God forbid your father should realize it. And I was almost a woman then, older than the other kids in the class. I'd missed so much school after the war that they sent me down to a lower grade.

As the alarm exploded in our ears, Mr. Emmitt stopped what he was saying about comma splices and sighed. Everyone around me laughed for some reason, and one boy even cheered. I was wild—it was not Philadelphia anymore to me. It was the UNRWA school in the camp, and everyone was frightened, but calmly scuttling underneath their desks, chests heaving. Huda used to chew on the end of her braid, and I wished I could do that now, realizing how it must have comforted her. But my hair had all been chopped off weeks ago. God save us, we actually used to think that this technique—hiding under the desks—would protect us from the bombs. But, *y'allah*, what did we know?

I became angry too, when the alarm sounded, because nobody seemed upset, not even Mr. Emmitt. And I was angry because I had been promised by Mama, on the airplane to Philadelphia, as I violently chewed gum the stewardess had given me to keep my ears from bursting, that we would be safe in our new home. And look what was happening, on my very first day! So I decided to save myself. I wouldn't be killed with a smile on my face like these fools. When you grow up in the camps and you see what I used to see—when you have a friend you tell your secrets to, and then a missile lands on her home, or the soldiers drag her into the shrubs as she walks home from school, then what? Then you learn to survive. Do you know this word, *survive*?

Everyone lined up at the front of the room, but I crashed through the door, into the hallway, and ran. The alarm was louder in the hallway and my chest started quaking, and I couldn't breathe fully, couldn't fill my lungs. But I still ran. Other people stepped out into the hallway, keeping in their useless lines, but I barely saw them because I was looking, of course, for a place to hide.

And then I saw it—an open door, and I ran in, and closed it. I pushed everything I could find in front of it, like a blockade; I used buckets, carts, cans, even a mop handle that I slid between the two bolts on the door. If soldiers planned to storm this place, I thought, sliding down to the ground and gathering my knees to my chest, they would have to take me after a battle.

Baba had promised that we wouldn't have to run anymore. He came to our home, back in the camp one day, and his face was sad. Even when he told us he had managed finally—after four years—to get us visas to the United States, we couldn't believe that we were leaving the camp. We were lucky, and we knew it. We could only get out because Baba's cousin, who had gone to America in 1948, made some papers for him. It had never been our home—Haifa would always be our real home—but still . . . I thought of Dina down the alley, whose father had died when they bombed the olive groves one day, and her stepbrother who hobbled to a bus every day on his crutches—his right leg lost to a landmine—to work at a candy factory in the city. Dina used to come to my room and cry sometimes. Her stepbrother was frustrated with his condition, knowing he couldn't get married, because girls needed husbands who could provide for them, and who could he provide for by wrapping little silver papers on chocolate for ten hours a day? Well, he was frustrated. And I guess he tried once or twice to . . . *you know what I am saying?—yes, I can see you know.* So he tried with Dina. And she was scared to death. How could I leave her in that house, with nobody to help her hide? At least she could tell her mother she was sleeping at my house, but now that I was going to America, where soldiers didn't break into your house and landmines didn't steal your brother's legs . . . Where would she go? Even now, I wonder what happened to her.

I shouldn't talk about Dina anymore. I don't want to.

No, I will not. It's not my right to tell her story. I can only tell you mine.

You? You can tell mine because I am giving it to you to keep safe, or to tell all the people, or to tell your sociology professor. Do as you like. It is yours now.

Where was I?

Yes. The closet. How was I to know it was a janitor's closet? To me, it was like the bunkers in the camp. There was water, and even some crackers and juice boxes on a shelf above the toilet scouring powder. Heaven!

We had landed two weeks before this in the United States, but I already felt like a survivor. I was worried about your aunt and uncles, who were all in the middle school. I was in the high school building, and I wondered if they had found a place to hide as well. I went to the little sink and threw up, then huddled down on the floor again, my stomach twisting with fear.

It was like the day at the orange grove in Haifa, the day it all happened. Maybe it wasn't when the problems started, but it was when I began to understand. Most of the Palestinians in Haifa were thrown out in 1948, but Baba managed to return after the war. Even so, by the time I was born, nothing was certain. Our life was temporary, like we always knew they would come for us one day. If we didn't eat our food, Mama would always threaten us, "The soldiers will come for you." I remember your grandparents always seemed worried. My father always had a frown on his face, making his mouth look like a scar, and my mother started practicing in secret how to shoot a gun. I found her and my uncle Fouad one day—Fouad was her youngest brother, the one who died in 1982— behind the house when Baba was in the fields. Uncle Fouad's *hatta* waved in the breeze around his head. It was always pure white, because he washed his own clothes and took care of his appearance. I thought he looked like a prince when he sat on his horse, his reddish-brown stallion with the white streak between his eyes.

On this day, Uncle Fouad was helping my mother point a shotgun at a box on top of the white stone fence on our land. "Aim properly," he was saying in his gentle voice. "If you watch it as you fire, you will hit it."

I giggled then, from the sheer delight of seeing my handsome uncle, and hoping he would take me for a ride on his horse. But when I giggled, Mama shot the gun prematurely and the blast frightened me so much that I started crying, humiliated to be doing so in front of my uncle, but scared anyway.

Mama yelled at me for sneaking around, and warned me not to tell my father. I stood there, still sobbing, when Uncle Fouad offered to give me a ride around on the fields. I clapped excitedly, and let him hoist me up in the saddle.

"Why is Mama playing with the gun?" I asked, feeling the wind in my hair.

"To protect you from the Zionists," he responded calmly. He never lied to me, the way the other adults did, and I adored him. That's his picture there, in the small frame, the black and white photo. See how white his *hatta* is? He refused to leave the camp with us, and he broke your grandmother's heart when he died, because she used to take care of him like her own son.

Weeks after I saw my mother with the gun, I heard her screaming for me and my brother and sisters. We ran back to the house, and my skirt and pockets were filled with oranges from the grove. Mama and Baba were frantically packing some clothes and money and loading them onto the old mules we owned. I saw Mama stuff her gold—her bracelets, necklaces, and rings, in the front of her *thawb*, near her bosom.

We started to walk, and I thought we would never stop. Seven of us trudged on, and sometimes I helped Mama carry Rabe—your uncle was just a baby then—and keep Ihab, Rana, and Samia in line and cheerful as we marched. Sometimes, I would wake up and realize that Baba was carrying me. For the first few days, we still had some of our oranges with us, and we would peel them and eat them, and then lick the juice from our fingers. The smell of the oranges got on my dress and on my skin and I smelled it the whole time we walked. We didn't ask what was going on. I thought if I kept eating my oranges, they would stop coming for us, but when I said this out loud, your grandparents' frowns shut me up.

Do you know that I sat in that janitor's closet, and even though I knew that the pine cleaner odor surrounded me, I still smelled fresh oranges? It's impossible, logically, but I tell you that it filled my nostrils, that scent, and the back of my tongue prickled. In the camp we ended up in, I used to smell it. Even now—how many years later?—I can still smell it, and I remember it all—Dina huddling on my mattress, Huda chewing on her hair, Uncle Fouad riding the horse with the white streak between its eyes, Mama stuffing gold in her bosom, and me, hiding under a UNRWA desk, hiding in a closet, hoping something would shield me from what was to be, from the soldiers, the bombs, the devil. Everyone.

Who knows how long I was in that closet? Maybe two hours? And then I heard voices on the speakers—the principal Mr. Green, telling me to come out, wherever I was. That same morning, my first day of school in America, and he said to me, "How are you, young man?" Can you imagine? I guess he didn't know that Huda was a girl's name, but I was humiliated. Mama had chopped all our hair when we left the camp to come to America, the way your grandfather used to shear the sheep in Haifa, because we all had hair down to our hips and it was expensive to wash and care for here, and Mama never had time anymore. I remember how we cried, even Mama cried, and Baba threw his hands up in the air, asking, "Are you all Samsons? Lost your strength now? We lost everything, and this is what you cry for?" That first day in school, I was also wearing trouser pants and a long T-shirt that said "Philadelphia Phillies" on the front—donated by a kind neighbor—so maybe I really did look like a boy.

Mr. Emmitt's voice came on the loudspeaker too, darling Mr. Emmitt, who asked me to please come out and it would be alright. My UNRWA English served me well enough to understand that much, but I would not leave. I remember the stories of soldiers holding a gun to people's heads and making them speak to get their relatives out of a house. I was not stupid. I snacked on the crackers I found, and they settled my stomach a bit. Much later, I heard another voice—that of my mother—telling me in Arabic, "*Habibti*, come out. It really is OK." I trusted only her voice.

And of course, I ran out, kicking the buckets and mops and brooms out of my way, flying down the hallway, when another teacher spotted me—they had all been looking for me—and took me to the big office where my mother was. The first thing I asked was if Ihab, Rana, and Samia were OK, and she said they were fine. Mr. Green and Mr. Emmitt then explained to me what a fire drill was, and I felt miserable. So humiliated.

They let me return home, rather than finish the day. It was better anyway, because everyone in school now knew who I was—the new girl with the short haircut, who was older than everyone else and barely spoke English. The skinny boy who really was a girl. The kid who hid in the janitor's closet because the fire drill scared her. The girl whose mother had to come to school and talk to her on the speaker in a funny language that sounded like spitting.

How's that, Reema? Enough material for your stories? When I went back? Well, it was not fun. Some of the classmates looked at me strangely, and many laughed. One girl told everyone I was dirty because I was wearing the same Phillies shirt, but in the camp, we wore the same clothes two or three days in a row unless we got dirty or sweated in them. But I never made that mistake in this country again. Your father always asks me why I buy so many clothes. "Just leave me alone on this issue," I tell him.

But the first day back, a Korean girl smiled at me, and she sat with me during lunch. I don't even remember her name now, but she was very petite and very pretty and she used to twirl her hair with her fingers all the time. She moved to a different school the next year, but for the rest of that first year, she was my friend and she knew some English. It was nice. I was grateful. We sat together and read the same books and I even visited her in her home once, with your grandmother. Our mothers couldn't even say a word to each other, but they just smiled and made these gestures and exaggerated faces, listening to our giggles. Three languages existed in that room, and my friend and I were the only ones who knew more than one. Our English wasn't great, but it's like a bridge. As long as it gets you safely to the other side, what else matters?

I have to finish dinner now. OK? Good. Just shape the words I said the way you want—fix them and make them sound good. You are the writer, habibti, *not me.*

About the Author

Susan Muaddi Darraj is associate professor of English at Harford Community College in Bel Air, Maryland. She edited *Scheherazade's Legacy: Arab and Arab American Women on Writing,* which was published by Praeger Press in 2004. Her fiction, essays, and articles have appeared in several publications and anthologies. She is also the Senior Editor of *The Baltimore Review.*